PURRFECT DATE

THE MYSTERIES OF MAX 47

NIC SAINT

PURRFECT DATE

The Mysteries of Max 47

Edited by Chereese Graves

www.nicsaint.com

Give feedback on the book at: info@nicsaint.com

facebook.com/nicsaintauthor
@nicsaintauthor

First Edition

Printed in the U.S.A

PURRFECT DATE

A Confederacy of Daters

When the well-known and popular dating site Valina Fawn was hacked, and a list of its members leaked online, a lot of people got into a lot of trouble. Men whose wives had no idea of their adulterous ways, wives whose men were surprised at their popularity with the other sex. And as luck would have it, the three men in our family were also on that fateful—or faithless—list, causing Odelia, Marge and Charlene to call an urgent family meeting.

So when Valina Fawn herself, after whom the site had been named, was found murdered, it's safe to say there was no lack of possible suspects. Was it a jilted wife? A cheating husband? A frustrated investor? Fortunately they could always call 911, where they would be greeted by the sultry tones of Gran or Scarlett, who'd both been engaged as the new dispatchers. Though their peculiar ideas on how to fill the role soon caused tongues to wag.

And then there was Harriet, who, after accidentally swiping right on Pettr, the popular dating site for pets, was being pursued by a sparrow, of all species. Brutus wasn't happy about it, feeling the sting even more when the sparrow turned out to be no mean serenader.

CHAPTER 1

It was book club night at Tex and Marge's place—though Tex was conveniently elsewhere, since he wasn't a member—and the house was cozily busy. Marge, as Hampton Cove's librarian, did the honors as usual, in the sense that she picked the book, sent out the invitations and supplied the necessary refreshments for the participants, and I must say she did a great job.

Her daughter Odelia was there, of course, and so was our mayor, Charlene Butterwick. The other members were unknown quantities as far as I was concerned, but I still viewed them with the kind benevolence of a cat who knows that treats will be forthcoming and cuddles given—all in moderation, of course.

The book Marge had chosen was *Tears in the Mud* by Jacqueline B. Wilding, a torrid tome of love and loss, and clearly the participants had all enjoyed the book tremendously, as evidenced by the glowing comments they awarded it.

All in all, as far as I could tell, book club was mostly an excuse to get together and gossip, while enjoying free cake, tea and cookies, but then who am I? Just a lowly feline observer that nobody pays too much attention to—apart from said treats and cuddles.

Book club membership currently stood at eight. Which meant that apart from Marge, Odelia and Charlene, five other ladies had decided to show up. They were, reading from left to right: Emma Kulhanek, who was a sort of mousy-looking housewife, Lynnette Say, also a housewife, but more of the glamorous '*The Real Housewives of New York City*' type, Adra Elfman, an elderly lady who was also a regular at the library, Carlotta Brook, who ran our local archery club and was allegedly a crack shot with bow and arrow, and of course the rising star in our local business community: the one and only Valina Fawn.

You may have heard of Valina. You may even have signed up for the dating site she runs, also called Valina Fawn, and one of the better-known and successful dating sites out there right now. Forget about Tinder or OkCupid or any of those highfaluting apps. Valina Fawn is the site both the loveless and the hopeful all turn to when looking for love.

"Is it true that the President himself found the First Lady on your site, Valina?" asked Adra Elfman now. The old lady sat nibbling a chocolate chip cookie and looking at Valina with delight. It wasn't too much to say that one of the main reasons Marge's book club meetings were so popular lately was exactly because of Valina's star quality. Though of course the lady knew discretion was key, and kept her trade secrets very much to herself.

"That would be telling, Adra," said Valina, who was a strikingly handsome woman in her early forties. Her straight blond hair was coiffed to perfection, and as usual she was dressed in one of her trademark power suits. "And as you know, a lady never tells."

"So it's true," Adra murmured, her eyes shining brightly.

"I very much doubt whether the President found his wife on a dating site," said Lynnette. "I'm sure he's got better things to do than to trawl those awful sites—no offense, Valina."

"None taken," said Valina graciously. She knew better than most that the notion of finding love on the internet still carried a certain stigma, and worked hard to erase it.

"It's exactly because the President has so many things on his mind that he doesn't have time to go out and find himself a partner," said Emma Kulhanek. "The man is so busy all the time I can easily imagine how he would turn to a dating site to find love again." She smiled a little smile as she demurely crossed her fingers in her lap. "In fact I think you're providing a wonderful service, Valina. To bring people together is an act of compassion."

Lynnette glanced over to Emma. For some reason the two ladies had never got on. Perhaps because Lynnette saw herself reflected in Emma, though in a more banal way. "You would say that, Emma," she said. "You're exactly the kind of person Valina caters to."

Emma frowned. "And what kind of person is that, may I ask?"

"Well, the hopeless romantic, of course."

"There's nothing wrong with being romantic," now Charlene piped up. "In fact it's romance that provides a glimmer of hope for humanity."

"Which brings us right back to our book," said Marge, managing a nice segue.

"Didn't you and Valina go to school together, Emma?" asked Carlotta Brook. The archery club's chairwoman was tall and boyishly coiffed, and had at one time been a professional archer, even going so far as to earn herself an Olympic medal in her chosen discipline. She still had the sinewy athleticism that had served her so well, as well as the no-nonsense attitude.

"Yes, we did," said Valina, who'd been checking her phone. "Seems like such a long time ago now, doesn't it, Em?"

Emma smiled. "It certainly does. Though having kids of my own, it all seems to come back to me. Especially since they're going to the same school we went to. Though it's all quite different now, of course. Especially since I'm teaching at the very school I was a student at."

"Hard to credit that you're both the same age," said Lynnette, glancing from Emma to Valina. "You seem so... different."

Emma's smile wavered. "If you're trying to tell me I look old, you can come right out and say it, Lynnette. No need to beat about the bush."

"Ladies, ladies," said Odelia, holding up her hands like a referee. "We're all friends here. All united in our appreciation of fine literature?"

There were murmurs of agreement, though judging from the looks Emma was shooting in Lynnette's direction, it was clear that the latter's insensitive remarks would be addressed at a later date.

"Is it true that George Clooney found his Amal through your site?" asked Adra, who'd dipped in and had secured herself another chocolate chip cookie. The old lady clearly was more interested in any gossip Valina was willing to dispense than in fine literature.

"That would be telling, now wouldn't it?" said Valina finely.

"George doesn't need a dating site," said Carlotta. "That man had to fend off the women throwing themselves at his feet back in the day. With all the ladies vying for his attention he could have started a dating site on his own, with him the only male."

"Is there anyone here who actually found love through a dating site?" asked Lynnette. "And it doesn't have to be Valina's site, though of course hers is the Rolls Royce of sites." She gave the businesswoman an ingratiating look. "I'll go first, shall I?" she immediately added. "I responded to some of those dating ads in the paper once—your paper, actually, Odelia—but unfortunately found them slim pickings. The men I ended up going out with were all horribly uncouth, I must say." She slightly tilted her chin. "Dross of mankind."

"So how did you find Franco?" asked Charlene, referring to Lynnette's husband.

"Quite the old-fashioned way, actually," said Lynnette. "We bumped into each other at a fundraiser for orphaned kids. He had just bid on a marvelous Willem de Kooning, and I had bid on an amazing Jackson Pollock, and when we went backstage to make the necessary arrangements, we got to talking. His views on life and art perfectly matched with mine, and so when he asked if I wanted to see his art collection, of course I said yes."

"You're sure he was referring to his art collection and not something else?" said Emma.

Lynnette shot a look that could kill in her fellow book club member's direction and shrugged. "You don't have to tell us how you met your hubby, Em. I'm sure it's a story so saccharine it'll make our teeth hurt."

"It wasn't through a dating site, if that's what you mean," said Emma, bridling a little. "But it was a romantic tale, that's true. When our school needed a new online learning platform, Norwell was the man in charge of design and construction. So we got to work together very closely indeed. And during one of those late-night meetings I suddenly realized that I was looking forward to seeing him much more than I should. And as he later admitted, he felt exactly the same way. Three months later we were married."

"And how about you, Odelia?" asked Valina. "How did you and Chase meet?"

"Through work, I guess," said Odelia. "He was this cocky cop who'd joined our local police force and hated me meddling in police affairs. So we ended up crossing swords quite a lot, even as we tackled some of the most baffling murder cases. But once I saw past his cockiness, and he got down from his high horse... Well, we just hit it off."

"Oh, how romantic!" Adra cried. "And so much more interesting than discussing a boring book, wouldn't you say?"

"Odd that they would get together for book club and think talking about books is boring," said Dooley, who was lying on the couch next to me.

"I'm sure they'll get around to discussing the book eventually," I said, though clearly Marge wasn't holding out hope, as evidenced by the fact that she'd already put her copy of the book down and was sitting back, resigned to listen to stories about first meets.

"I guess when you and Tex first met dating sites weren't around yet, were they?" asked Lynnette, addressing their fearless book club leader.

"Not sites as such," said Marge, "though just like you I did respond to an ad in the paper. Though when I say responded, it would probably be closer to the truth to say that my mom responded and then guilted me into going. You see, I'd just broken up with my boyfriend, and was feeling a little down in the dumps, and Ma thought I needed cheering up."

"Mom!" said Odelia. "You never told me you met dad through a personal ad."

"Well, I did," said Marge. "He was a medical student back then, and one of his fellow students had actually sent in that ad, so when he showed up for our date he was less than excited, feeling he had to go through with it, or be accused of being disloyal. And since I felt exactly the same, it wasn't a propitious start. But much to our surprise, we hit it off immediately, and have been together ever since." She smiled at the recollection. "Though I'm not sure my mother still doesn't regret setting us up for that date."

"Are you kidding?" said Charlene. "Any mother would kill to see her daughter go off and marry a doctor."

"I know, but my previous boyfriend was the son of a local millionaire businessman, so in my mother's view a mere doctor was a step down in my fortunes. Though I never saw it that way. Also, my former boyfriend is in prison now for kidnapping his own wife, so it's safe to say my mother's views on him have since gone through a major modification."

They all laughed at this, but then Valina's phone chimed and she got up. "I'm sorry, but I have to take this," she murmured, and hurried off into the kitchen. We heard her talking rather heatedly into her phone, but then as more people shared the details of their love life with the others, we forgot all about Valina and her urgent call. Until, that is, she came hurrying back into the living room to grab her coat. "I have to go, Marge," she said, shooting a look of apology in the latter's direction. "Something came up at the office."

And without further ado, she shot out of the room like a flash.

"What kind of an emergency can there be with a dating app?" asked Carlotta laughingly.

"A bad match?" joked Charlene.

"Or maybe the site has gone haywire," said Lynnette. "And people are all being forced to swipe left when they want to swipe right. Or is it the other way around? I'm not well-versed in the latest minutiae of dating, and glad of it, too, if you want to know." She performed an exaggerated eye roll. "I'm just happy I found my perfect match before the days of internet dating became the hype *du jour*. It all seems so complicated now!"

"Doesn't it just," said Adra. She held up her hand and flicked her wedding ring. "Been married fifty years this autumn. Hard to believe it's been that long."

"So how did you and Gene meet, Adra?" asked Carlotta.

The old lady's eyes flickered. "In a book club just like this one, only a slightly saucier one I must admit. It was one of those underground book clubs that focused on the racy kind of book. Most of the members were women, of course, but there was one brave soul who'd ventured into the unknown, though he was under the impression it was a Jane Austen book club. Until he discovered the kind of books we were reading. He gamely went along, though, and soon was the center of attention, of course. The only man in a club full of women. Later on he told me that he liked me from the first. And I must say I fancied him, too. Especially since he had such a nice voice when he read out those long erotic passages from *Lady Chatterley's Lover*!"

More laughter filled the room, and I slowly drifted off to sleep.

Marge's book club members may love to share stories of first love, but frankly the only story I'm interested in is the story of my perfect couch. Talk about love at first sight!

CHAPTER 2

By the time I opened my eyes again, all book club members had mercifully dispersed, and Marge and Odelia were gathering cups and saucers and carrying them into the kitchen. A strange sound reached my ears, and when I looked over, I saw that Harriet was sitting nearby, hovering over a tablet computer and deftly swiping it with her paw pads. The sound that had roused me from my nice nap was Harriet quietly but with rising intensity saying, "No, no, no, no, no! How is this possible!"

I gave her a lazy look. "What's wrong?"

"Oh, it's this new dating app," the pretty white Persian said. "I can't make heads nor tails of the thing."

Dooley had to laugh at this. "Heads nor tails," he said. "Funny." When Harriet shot him a withering glance, he weekly added, "Tails. Because you have a tail?"

"Oh, Dooley," Harriet grumbled, then frowned some more at her tablet.

Brutus, who'd wandered into the kitchen, looking for a bite to eat, now returned. "Stay out of the kitchen," he said. "It never ceases to amaze me how people who love books can make such a mess. Marge and Odelia have been doing the dishes for what feels like hours."

"It's because Marge likes to show off by taking out her finest China," I explained. "And since she can't put them in the dishwasher they all have to be washed by hand. And with special detergent that doesn't cause any damage. And all hand-dried very carefully and replaced in the cupboard, lest they might chip."

Brutus had hopped up onto the couch next to his mate and now frowned at the tablet. "What is this?" he asked.

"Nothing special, sweetie," said Harriet. "Just some app I'm trying out."

"Is that... Pettr?" asked Brutus, sounding aghast.

"What's Pettr?" I asked.

"It's like Tinder for pets," Brutus explained. "You swipe right when you have a match." He now took a closer look at the app his lady love was surfing on. "It *is* Pettr. Why are you on Pettr?" he demanded.

"I was just curious, sugar babe," said Harriet. "Shanille told me about it, and so I wanted to take a look. Just to know what all the fuss was about."

"Shanille is on Pettr?" asked Brutus.

"Yeah, she is."

"What is a dating app, Max?" asked Dooley.

"It's an app where people looking for a partner find each other," I said.

"How does it work, exactly?"

"Well, you create a profile on the site or the app, with a picture that was taken twenty years ago, then you write something about yourself, usually painting yourself in a more favorable light, and then you hope that someone who comes across your profile likes it enough to swipe right and give you a try. And if you like the person who swiped right, you can also swipe right and you arrange to meet."

"So you don't look like you, and write stuff that isn't really you, and the other person does the same?" said Dooley, catching on quickly.

"That's about the gist of it," I agreed.

"But won't the other person notice that you lied?"

"Of course they will, but you hope that social pressure will prevent them from walking out on you in the middle of a busy restaurant, and that through the sheer magnetism of your personality you'll be able to make them forget you're twenty years older and thirty pounds heavier, and that you're not as fascinating as you made out to be in your profile."

"Sounds like a recipe for disaster," was my friend's estimation.

"And yet sometimes it seems to works," I said.

"And sometimes it doesn't," said Harriet, and gave us all a sad look. "I accidentally swiped right when I should have swiped left. So now what?"

"Now you're going on a date," I said cheerfully.

"What?!" Brutus cried. "No way!"

"I'm sorry, sunshine," said Harriet. "I got confused."

"Between left and right?!" he asked, incredulous.

"I mix up left and right all the time," said Dooley.

"So who did you match with?" asked Brutus. Then, as he took a closer look, he gasped in shock. "No way!"

"Who is it?" I asked, my curiosity aroused in spite of myself. But all I got were blank looks from both Harriet and Brutus.

"It'll be fine," said Brutus. "You simply stand him up, that's all."

"It's not going to be good for my rating," Harriet said.

"Who cares about your rating!" He eyed her suspiciously. "Unless you want to keep on dating?"

"Of course not, snuggle bear! Like I said, I was just taking a look."

"That's fine, then," said Brutus, though he didn't seem entirely convinced. Then again, if I found my girlfriend creating a profile on a dating site, I wouldn't be convinced of her innocence in the matter either.

"Is Pettr the same site our humans were talking about earlier?" asked Dooley.

"No, that was the human version. It's called Valina Fawn," I said. "Named after the site's founder and president Valina Fawn."

"It's so interesting to have a real celebrity in our midst," said Dooley now, as he placed his head on his front paws. "So did she really set George Clooney up with Amal?"

Oh, God. What was the world coming to when even Dooley was starting to spread celebrity gossip?

Just then, there was a loud crashing sound coming from the kitchen, followed by irate voices. Moments later, Tex walked into the living room. His face was red and he had a hunted look on his face. "Who puts their best China on a table in front of the kitchen door?" he muttered, then sank down on the nearest couch and turned on the television. A dating show was in full progress, so he decidedly flipped the channel until he'd landed on the Discovery Channel, which was showing a documentary about the migratory pattern of the native geese. Tex relaxed and moments later was in a deep sleep, and so were we.

CHAPTER 3

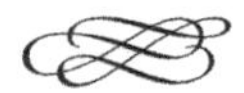

On Saturday morning at the Brookwell Archery Club, three familiar figures were having a whale of a time. They were Tex Poole, his son-in-law Chase Kingsley, and Tex's brother-in-law Alec Lip. All three men were holding bow and arrow, but so far they hadn't exactly been successful in hitting their targets, which had been set up a little ways away—at any rate too far away for them to hit them. Then again, they probably would have had a hard time hitting anything unless it was three feet away.

Archery is a demanding sport, after all, and only through diligent practice can one hope to get any good at it. And since the only reason Tex, Chase and Alec were members of the club was because the price of the lukewarm beer they served in the clubhouse was the best price in town, they didn't stand a chance of ever going to the Olympic Games.

Carlotta Brook herself was there, of course, and so was Carlotta's husband Dennis, who was in charge of the club's financial side: collecting membership fees and such. And it was with exactly this important task in mind that he now set foot for Alec Lip and discreetly led the police chief away from the others.

"I see you haven't paid your fees yet this month, Alec," Dennis said, lowering his voice when discussing this oh-so-delicate matter with the errant member in question. "If you're having trouble, we could maybe set up a payment plan? Easy weekly installments?"

"That won't be necessary," Alec grunted, looking a little annoyed. "Just a minor oversight, that's all." And when the other man stared at him, he added, with a touch of incredulity. "Surely you don't want me to pay you now, Dennis?"

"If you could. You can call me nitpicky, but I like everything to be just so."

"Oh, all right," said Alec, and took out his wallet to pay the man. He quickly glanced over, but both Tex and Chase had discreetly turned their heads the other way. No one likes to intervene in a close relative's financial affairs. That way only trouble and strife lie.

Once Tex had settled up, he rejoined the others, and as they stood sipping from their lukewarm beers, and idly gazing at the target somewhere in the distance, they talked about this and that, happy for this chance to shoot the breeze and strengthen those all-important bonds of friendship.

"So book club last night, huh?" said Chase. "How was it? Odelia wouldn't tell me."

"Plenty of gossip, from what I understand," said Tex. "Emma Kulhanek and Lynnette Say locked horns again, and Adra Elfman wanted to know how the others had all met their significant other. Marge was annoyed, I can tell you that much. She spends a lot of time preparing for these weekly meetings, and when all is said and done, nobody reads the book, nobody is interested in discussing the book, and the only thing she takes away from the meeting is the minutiae of everyone's love life, which isn't exactly the point."

"I'll bet it's more interesting than the book itself," said Alec with a grin. "Why did Emma and Lynnette lock horns?"

"Lynnette seems to think Emma is too dowdy for book club. She wants to raise book club's profile, and Emma isn't a good fit. With Charlene she has the mayor, Marge is a doctor's wife, Odelia is a prominent reporter, Carlotta is an Olympian and plays an important role in the local community as a Rotary Club member, and of course runs the archery club, and then there's Valina Fawn, who's a major celebrity in her own right."

"So where does Adra Elfman fit in?" asked Chase. "She's hardly a celebrity."

"Adra's husband Gene was the long-time chairman of the Chamber of Commerce," said Alec. "And he's still very well connected, even though he's now retired, of course."

"But isn't Emma's husband something big with Valina Fawn's site?" asked Chase.

"Norwell is a developer," said Tex. "So in Lynnette's eyes he's a computer geek."

"He's more than just a developer," said Alec. "Norwell is Valina's business partner."

"And Emma is a teacher, which isn't the kind of person Lynnette wants to be seen associating with," said Tex, shrugging his shoulders.

"In other words, Lynnette Say is a big, fat snob," said Chase.

"A snob with a lot of money, and since Marge is always on the lookout for people interested in donating to her library..."

Just then, Chase's phone chimed, and he took it out. He frowned at the display. "Did you guys see this? Looks like Valina Fawn has been hacked."

"Valina Fawn or her site?" asked Tex.

"The site." Chase's frown deepened. "Uh-oh. The hackers have put a list with the names of all of Valina Fawn's customers online."

And as they glanced around, suddenly phones of other members started beeping frantically. And as men took out their phones, faces blanched, muttered curses were uttered, strangled cries emitted, and before long a minor stampede was in motion, with people hurrying off to the parking lot and making a hasty departure.

When the dust had finally settled, the only ones left were Tex, Alec and Chase… and of course Carlotta and Dennis Brook. Though the latter looked very much ill at ease as he came face to face with his wife.

Carlotta stared at her husband with ill-concealed rage displayed on her sinewy face. Then she hauled off and hit him squarely in the stomach and walked off on a huff.

Dennis, who'd doubled up and staggered back, now stared at the departing image of his wife, his hand massaging his injured midsection, clearly stunned by this development.

Alec shook his head. "I just hope this won't lead to any problems," he said.

"Pretty sure it will," said Chase, and drained the last of his beer. He frowned when his own phone chimed, and took it out. "Family meeting—now!" he read from the display. He looked up to find both his father-in-law and uncle-in-law gazing at their own phones.

All three men shared a look.

The trouble had begun.

CHAPTER 4

A family meeting was called and took place in Marge and Tex's home. In the same living room where the day before Valina Fawn had been called away on some unspecified emergency—which I guess it's safe to say we now knew was the big leak her site had sprung—three men were being grilled to within an inch of their lives by the respective women in those lives.

"That's not me," said Chase blankly when he was confronted with the evidence. It was a bold defense, and I was certainly not a little bit curious if he'd be able to back it up. "No, I swear. I never signed up for that site," he assured an irate-looking Odelia. "Whoever put that picture of me on that damn dating site definitely has got some explaining to do."

"I don't know, Chase," said Odelia. "Former NYPD cop? Likes to work out and spoil his lady love? Must love dogs? It all sounds very much like you."

"Oh, honey, Chase would never do such a thing," said Marge. "The man is about to become a father for the first time. Which can't be said about you, Tex. What were you thinking!"

"I was just curious, honey!" Tex cried. "With all the hullabaloo around the site, I just wanted to see what all the fuss was about. I was never going to do any actual dating."

"You're cheating on my daughter," said Gran, "which means you're cheating on me. And frankly I think you should just kick him out, honey. Once a cheater, always a cheater."

"You can't throw me out of my own house, Vesta," said Tex tersely.

"Oh, yes, we can. Just do it, honey," she told her daughter. "It's one small step for you, but a giant leap for all womankind. Go on, or do you want me to do the honors?"

Meanwhile, Charlene sat eyeing her boyfriend with a cold eye. "I don't get it," the Mayor said. "You could have told me you weren't happy, Alec. We could have talked about it. But instead you went behind my back and—"

"I already told you—I just wanted to trap the Black Widow!"

"Oh, is that the code name she uses? So what does she look like, this secret girlfriend of yours? Do I know her?"

"The Black Widow is a known criminal," said Alec. "She's already killed five men, and rumor has it that she's in Hampton Cove right now, living under an alias. The FBI has credible intel she's on Valina Fawn, which is how she managed to lure her victims to their death, and so I just figured I'd try to find her by creating a profile and drawing her out!"

"A likely story," Charlene scoffed.

"It's the truth!"

"So what have we got?" said Gran. "One man who claims he's the victim of identity theft, another who just wanted to see 'what all the fuss was about' and a third who's looking for a black widow." She tsk-tsked lightly. "I call bullshit." And when cries of disagreement rose up, she repeated, louder this time, "Absolute bullshit!"

"What do you think, Max?" asked Dooley. "Do you think they're telling the truth?"

"Oh, absolutely," I said. "Though of course you can never really know for sure."

"There's one way to find out if Chase is telling the truth, at least," said Brutus. "Talk to the people who designed the site and ask them if they can check who created that profile."

"True," I said. "But then you'd have to get a warrant, and I doubt any judge would grant one based on the suspicion of a local reporter. No, I think Odelia, Marge and Charlene are just going to have to take their significant others' word for it, hard as that might be."

And as far as I could tell, it would be quite a while before that happened. And since none of us enjoys these family feuds, we decided to head out through the pet flap and take in some fresh air. Recriminations flying back and forth are not exactly my idea of a pleasant time to be had by all.

And we'd just left the house through the pet flap when a smallish bird suddenly materialized and stepped to the fore. He looked a little shy as he presented himself. "Hi, my name is Jack," said the bird, whom I immediately identified as belonging to the sparrow species. "And you must be Harriet," he added, and presented our friend with a small daisy he must have picked up in someone's backyard. "I'm glad to finally meet you, Harriet, and I can tell you right off the bat that I have a good feeling about this."

"A good feeling about what?" asked Harriet, as confused as the rest of us.

"This," said Jack, gesturing between himself and Harriet. "Our relationship."

Harriet's jaw dropped, and so did mine. Dooley merely gave the bird a look of keen interest. After having watched numerous nature documentaries, the mating ritual of birds holds no secrets for him. Brutus, meanwhile, was getting a little worked up.

"What do you mean, our relationship!" the butch black cat demanded heatedly.

"Well, you swiped right, and I swiped right, and of course that wasn't a big surprise, as I immediately felt this click, you know—a connection, if you see what I mean." The tiny bird smiled a diffident smile. "You must have felt the same, dearest Harriet. And now that I finally meet you in the flesh, as it were, I must say I'm not disappointed. On the contrary—you look even better in reality than on your profile, which is a rare thing these days."

A powerful rebuke had been trembling on Harriet's lips, but Jack's words took the wind out of her sails. "Oh," she said. "Do you really think so?"

"Absolutely. Gorgeous doesn't even begin to describe it."

"You've got some nerve!" Brutus cried, and took a menacing step in the direction of the small brown bird. Jack immediately took flight and settled in a nearby tree, where he was safe from our friend's sharp claws.

"Brutus, I'm sure this isn't necessary," said Harriet. "Jack is just trying to be nice."

"Nice!" Brutus cried. "He's talking about having a relationship with you!"

"I'm sorry to say that me swiping right was a mistake, Jack," Harriet now clarified. "I wanted to swipe left, but then something got in my eye, and I accidentally swiped right."

"What got in your eye was the fact that I'm the perfect partner for you, beautiful Harriet," said Jack, now causing us to have to look up, not down. "And I'm quite determined to prove it to you by showering you with my affections and my gifts."

"Gifts?" asked Harriet, perking up at this. "What gifts?"

"Harriet!" Brutus cried, exasperated. "He's a bird!"

"Well spotted, cat," said Jack. "I am indeed a bird. A love bird. And when you give me a chance, I'll make sweet, sweet love to you, morning, noon and night, lovely Harriet."

"Let me get at him," Brutus growled, and made to climb that tree. But unfortunately for him Jack took flight again, and this time perched on the gutter, from where he continued to give Harriet the glad eye. In fact he was winking at her, causing Harriet to giggle and Brutus to fume with righteous rage.

"You're sweet," Harriet said finally. "But I'm afraid this is one of those relationships that simply isn't to be, Jack."

"And why is that?" asked Jack. "I'm too short for you, is that it? Well, what I lack in height, I make up in honest heat. I can assure you that passion is my middle name."

"So his name is Jack Passion Sparrow?" asked Dooley.

"Something like that," I said.

"Jack the sparrow," said Dooley musingly. "Now what does that remind me of?"

"Brutus, come down from that drainpipe!" Harriet was yelling. But of course by the time Brutus finally reached the roof, Jack had flown off again, rerouting once again to that tree and making Brutus look really silly sitting up there on that roof.

"Looks like Brutus is stuck, Max," said Dooley.

"Yeah, looks like," I agreed.

"Don't just stand there!" Brutus cried. "Get me down from here!"

We turned when Jack suddenly started singing. Like a regular crooner, he was singing a love song, infusing it with all the warmth and fervor he harbored in his tiny bosom.

"Such a pity," Harriet murmured.

"What is?" I asked.

"That's he's just a sparrow and not some majestic bird of

prey. Like a bald eagle, you know, though of course if he were a bald eagle I'd ask him to get a toupee. Or a hair transplant. A cat of my stature can't be seen dating a baldie."

"He's a bird and you're a cat, Harriet," I said. "It wouldn't work."

"You don't know that," said Harriet. "Stranger things have happened. And besides, nobody's perfect."

"It's one of those impossible relationships, isn't it," said Dooley. "Like Romeo and Juliet, or Quasimodo and Demi Moore. Or even Emma Watson and the Beast."

"The Beauty and the Beast," Harriet murmured. "Now isn't that something?"

"Can someone get me down from here!" Brutus bellowed.

CHAPTER 5

Dolores Peltz had come down with a serious case of the flu, and since her only possible replacement was vacationing in Hawaii, doing one of those wild water rafting excursions and couldn't be reached, Chief Alec Lip had been forced to be creative, and had tasked his mother with taking over from Dolores for now. As Tex Poole's more-or-less faithful receptionist for many years, no one could fault Vesta with a lack of know-how. And as the leader of the neighborhood watch, she was intimately knowledgeable with both the town of Hampton Cove and the crime-fighting mindset. Plus, she'd been helping her granddaughter Odelia Poole and the latter's husband Chase Kingsley tackle many a difficult crime case, so she had some basic grasp of police procedure as well.

In other words: the perfect police dispatcher.

Vesta only had one proviso before she assumed the role: that her friend Scarlett Canyon was allowed to join her. As she explained it, being a police dispatcher was a stressful and lonely job, and she could use the company.

"I'm not sure," Alec had said, fingering one of his many

chins. But since he basically had no other choice, he finally caved to Vesta's demands.

And so it was that the women who called in to file an official complaint against Valina Fawn for leading their husbands astray, and the men who called in to file an official complaint against the site for being careless with their personal information, either had the misfortune of getting Vesta as their interlocutor, or Scarlett. It's safe to say that neither woman had a lot of compassion to dispense with.

"So your husband cheated on you," said Vesta. "Big deal. Dump him and get another one. I told my daughter exactly the same thing when we found out her husband is on that site: kick him out and start looking for a decent guy. Though I have to be honest with you, Mary, in my personal opinion all men are dogs, so I simply wouldn't bother if I were you. Just get a nice cat. Cats will never let you down. And I'm speaking from experience here."

"If you didn't want your personal information to leak," said Scarlett, seated next to Vesta, "you shouldn't have signed up for that site in the first place, Mike. What's wrong with simply meeting a potential partner in the frozen foods section at your local supermarket? Or at a local dance? It's not rocket science. Simply common sense."

They both hung up and took a breath. "Tough day," said Scarlett.

"Tell me about it."

They glanced at the switchboard. "Twenty calls waiting!" Scarlett cried. "No way!"

"If I'd known I'd have to work this hard, I wouldn't have taken the darn job."

Then they shrugged and simultaneously picked up their phones again. Duty called!

Valina Fawn wasn't having a good day. In fact she wasn't having a good week. First the news that her site had been hacked, and then the even worse news that the hackers had decided to dump the entire contents of their customer database online. The phones had been ringing off the hook, and they were facing a massive client exodus, which was understandable, since a major part of their appeal was a guarantee of client privacy.

And as if this wasn't all bad enough, now Norwell was giving her a bad time.

He was pacing her office, creeping back and forth like a crouching tiger—or a crouching pussycat, since Norwell was a full foot shorter than Valina. "I told you that security was one of your weak spots, Valina," Norwell was saying. "And you said you'd deal with it. Looks like you didn't 'deal with it' as much as ignore it—to your own detriment!"

"If you simply dropped by to tell me 'I told you so' I'll tell you right now to buzz off, Norwell," she said, swiveling annoyedly in her swivel chair, seated behind her comfortably large desk. When she'd started her own site, after having spent the formative years of her career setting up sites for other people, she'd sworn she'd get the biggest office with the biggest desk in the business, and she had. Tinder, Match, Pettr… Their CEOs all had much smaller desks. She knew, since she'd checked.

Norwell turned on her. "I came here to tell you we're in big, big trouble, Valina!"

"Tell me something I don't know."

"You know, I never thought I'd say this, but I sincerely regret ever having said yes to your proposal. I had a perfectly good job in Silicon Valley, with a perfectly comfortable pay packet, a great apartment, nice car, excellent schooling for my kids. And now what?"

"This is not the end, Norwell," she said emphatically, feeling that she better talk her business partner off the ledge or else he'd jump out of a window or under a train.

"It certainly looks like the end. We've lost thirty percent of our clientele. Thirty percent!"

"They'll come back," said Valina. "Once they realize we're still the best option in town to find the perfect partner."

"There's blood in the water!" said Norwell, flapping his arms like a chicken and going from concerned business partner to full-blown drama queen. "Our investors are going to drop us—banks are going to call in their loans. This is going to be bad. Very, very bad."

"Look, we're not the first business that got hacked. Others have survived, even thrived, and so will we. So we took a hit —we'll rally. The most important thing right now is to make sure we put measures in place that make us impregnable. And that's where you come in, Norwell."

"I knew this was going to happen," said Norwell, grabbing his head and going back to pacing back and forth. "The site is like a sieve. Anyone could have gotten in. Even some snot-nosed kid playing amateur hacker in his mom's basement could have hacked us."

"Then you better make sure you plug the hole," said Valina, quickly losing patience with the guy. "You need to get your act together, Norwell. And get the site back on track."

He stared at her for a moment, a sort of wild-eyed look in his eyes, then turned on his heel and left her office.

She breathed a sigh of relief. The last thing she needed right now was for the people the site depended on to lose their shit. Norwell Kulhanek had come highly recommended for his programming prowess, and since she'd always known that programming was the site's weak point, she'd wooed the man relentlessly, even going so far as to make him a partner, even though that went against the grain in every sense of the word.

Valina Fawn was her baby, a site she had nurtured and turned from a fledgling start-up into a juggernaut. And it was exactly that explosive growth that had caused a lot of teething problems. The infrastructure designed to carry a small site had quickly outgrown its usefulness, and since it's hard to redesign a site from the ground up when it's already up and running, she'd kept postponing the inevitable, until, apparently, it was too late.

Not too late, she chided herself. They'd recover from this disaster. They'd learn and grow and in due course regain people's trust, and it would be as if this hack had never happened.

Yeah, right. Who was she kidding!

CHAPTER 6

Odelia was in her editor's office, seated in front of the man's desk. Dan seemed particularly excited, as evidenced by the distinct waggle of his long white beard.

"This is the story of the century," the aged editor said. "We have to grab this thing and grab it good!"

"It just sounds like a lot of gossip to me," said Odelia. As she had always understood, Dan didn't want the *Hampton Cove Gazette* to turn into yet another gossip rag. Many times he had stressed that they had to be above that kind of tabloid journalism. And yet here it almost felt as if he was abandoning the principles of a lifetime for a juicy story. Then again, maybe the story was simply too big to ignore. Everyone was talking about it.

"It's not just idle gossip, Odelia," said Dan. "It's a human interest story. And it involves the whole community. Did you look at the list?"

"I did," she said, not wanting to point out that her own husband and her dad were on the list, not to mention her uncle.

"Everybody's on there! From the pharmacist to the

council member to businessmen, lawyers, shopkeepers, butchers, plumbers, celebrities... You name it and they're there!"

"I didn't see your name on the list," said Odelia.

"I'm too old for the dating game," he said with a wave of the hand. "But looks like the rest of the population isn't. So you go out there and you talk to as many people as you can. Cheated wives, husbands, boyfriends, girlfriends. Jilted lovers, cheated partners. We're going to cover this from every angle and go big on this story or go home. And I've already got the first interview lined up for you: Valina Fawn and Norwell Kulhanek have agreed to talk to the *Gazette* and only the *Gazette*. They won't be giving any other interviews."

"An exclusive, huh?"

"Absolutely. Me and Valina go way back. And also, she knows we'll treat this with dignity and respect. Now get out there and bring me back some exciting copy! Let's sell some papers!"

I don't usually protest when Odelia drags me and Dooley along on one of her interviews, but today I felt I needed to lodge an official protest. I'd just settled in for a nice nap on the couch she has installed in her office, and I didn't feel like traipsing off to talk to Valina Fawn about her site. I have this peculiar character defect, you see. I like to hunt down mysteries and solve them.

Whenever a murder is being committed in town, or some other crime, I'm usually to be found taking a first-row seat and gathering the facts of the matter. But this was no mystery. This was just a tawdry story about hackers hacking yet another site, the way we've all read dozens or maybe even hundreds of stories the last couple of years. Hackers hack, usually for financial gain, and nobody seems to be able to stop them.

"Do we have to go?" I asked now, not hiding my reluctance.

"Yes, we do," said Odelia sternly. "A crime was committed, Max. Don't you want to catch the people who are behind it?"

"What's the point?" I argued. "They're probably in Russia or China or North Korea, like all those hackers always seem to be. And since nobody can touch them, or bring them to justice, it all seems so utterly pointless, wouldn't you say?"

"No, I would not," said Odelia. "We have plenty of home-grown hackers, and if we can find out who they are, it's going to make a huge difference."

I grudgingly admitted she might have a point, and dragged myself up from my couch.

"You're like Nero Wolfe, Max," said Dooley as we followed Odelia out.

"How so?" I asked. As far as I know I don't have a strange predilection for orchids.

"Nero Wolfe is very choosy about which case he takes on, and so are you."

"Our time is precious, Dooley," I said. "And so we have to be selective." And also, I hadn't slept well last night. It seemed as if a lot of negative energy was buzzing through the air, centered around these horrendous dating sites. Harriet and Brutus had argued about Jack the sparrow, Tex and Marge about the doctor's presence on the site, and even Odelia and Chase had spent all night exchanging words that are not conducive to an atmosphere of peace and good will.

The offices of Valina Fawn were nice enough, dominated as they were by an orange-and-pink color scheme. I spotted a foosball table in the lounge, a ball bath and even a row of old-fashioned pinball machines. Clearly Valina held to the view shared by most Silicon Valley start-ups that to attract competent personnel, you have to treat them like five-year-olds.

Valina herself looked distraught, though she tried to hide it by plastering a big smile on her face when we walked into her office. She offered us herbal tea, or a special blend of coffee, or even organic lemonade, and Odelia opted for the latter. For us cats Valina's assistant brought in a dish of purified water, which was nice and cool to our tongues.

Once we'd taken a seat in a corner of Valina's office, seated on orange chairs with bright yellow cushions, a man joined us who she introduced as Norwell Kulhanek.

"Is he…" Dooley began.

"Emma Kulhanek's husband," I said.

Norwell was a compact man with a serious face and thick-framed, square glasses. He was clutching his phone as if it was a lifeline, and looked as reluctant to be there as I was.

"I don't have a lot of time," he said. "The site needs my attention, as you can imagine."

"Of course," said Odelia. "And I'm very grateful you wanted to sit down for this interview."

"Norwell isn't just my business partner," said Valina, "he's also the site's main programmer."

"Oh, so maybe you could tell us how these hackers managed to get access to your clients' data so easily," said Odelia, settling in with her organic lemonade and her tablet on her lap, stylus poised to take notes.

Norwell shot Odelia a look of extreme censure. "It's a complicated topic, I'm afraid. Very technical."

"I don't mind," said Odelia. "And I'm sure the *Gazette's* readers would like to know."

And so for the next fifteen minutes Norwell expounded on the kind of topic that would send just about anyone who isn't an absolute computer nerd into a coma. I have to admit

I tuned out after the first five minutes of his lengthy exposé. I confess I'm not much of a computer person, especially when you get down into the nitty-gritty of the thing.

"Are you sleeping, Max?" asked Dooley finally.

"Pretty much," I admitted.

"It's not going to be a very interesting interview, is it?"

"Not so much."

"I thought Odelia was going to cover the human interest angle, but instead she'll have to write an article that might be a better fit for *PC Magazine* than the *Gazette*."

And since I had the impression Norwell was only getting started, we wandered out into the corridor, to sniff up some of that local color that is so important for any journalist worth their salt, and in the meantime try and wrangle us some kibble in the process.

I mean, if the company hotshots don't mind bringing in ball baths and foosball tables, why not pets, too? I once read a story about a retirement home that keeps a goat on site. It has proven very enjoyable for the residents, as they get to pet said goat, and even feed it. Unfortunately it didn't take us long to discover a marked dearth of pets on the premises.

And we'd just concluded our investigation by taking a long hard look at the cafeteria when Valina and Norwell came breezing in. Ostensibly for a refill, but in actual fact Norwell seemed eager to dispense with a few home truths.

"I'm sorry, Valina, but if anyone is going down for this, it won't be me!"

"Nobody is going down," said Valina as she fiddled with the coffee machine. It was one of those machines you need a college degree to operate, with plenty of nobs and levers.

"The only reason I agreed to do the interview is because my lawyers want me to appear cooperative, but if it wasn't for that, I'd have been out of here already!"

"Oh, so now we're talking to our lawyers already, are we? I didn't realize we were at that stage."

"Wake up, Valina. We're long past that stage. All we can do now is damage control. And like I told you before, I'm not going to watch a reputation I spent my entire career building destroyed through your sheer and utter incompetence!" To add emphasis to his words, he was pointing a finger at the dating site owner, and stabbing it into her shoulder.

"*Your* reputation! What about *my* reputation? I created this site! It carries my name!"

"I don't care. It's every man for himself now as far as I'm concerned. If you need me, I'll be in the basement—trying to fix your screwup!"

"They're not exactly the best of friends, are they, Max?" said Dooley as we watched Norwell leave. He hadn't even refilled his cup.

"When the shit hits the fan, business partners rarely stay friends," I said. "Usually their relationship is more along the lines of rats leaving a sinking ship."

"Rats!" Dooley cried, jumping about a foot from the floor. "Where!"

"Proverbial rats, Dooley," I explained. "Not real ones."

"Oh, thank God. I don't like rats, Max."

"Who does?"

We decided to wander back to Valina's office to see if Odelia was still awake after this bombardment with technical jargon. "Do you think there are rats on Pettr, Max?"

"I doubt it," I said. "Who would want to date a rat?"

"Other rats?"

"I guess so," I said doubtfully. "Though rats aren't exactly known for their discernment and sense of good taste, are they? No doubt rats simply mate with the first mate they meet."

"I think there's probably a lot of things about rats that we don't know, Max. Maybe they're more romantic than we think. Like the rest of the animal kingdom they're capable of love and the finer emotions. For instance, I once heard that rats mate for life. But only the Californian rat."

"And why is that?"

"I don't know. Maybe it's got something to do with the weather?"

"Here is something I heard," I said. "Your average pair of rats can produce as much as half a billion offspring during their lifespan, which is usually three years."

"That's a lot of rats, Max," said Dooley with a shiver.

"And I can assure you, Dooley, that romance doesn't feature into the thing. For rats it's quantity over quality all the way."

And as we passed by an office marked 'Accounting' I found myself thinking that at Valina Fawn the same thing applied: the more people who signed up with the site, the more money ended up in the company coffers. For love or money? Evidently the latter.

CHAPTER 7

As far as I could tell, Odelia's interview had been a big bust, but when we were in the car, driving back to the office, she told us that there was at least one upshot. One takeaway she was particularly happy about.

"Turns out that Chase was telling the truth," she said as she steered her aged pickup along the road. "I talked to one of the people in charge of programming, and asked if he could tell if a person signing up was the actual person or simply someone using their name and picture. He looked at Chase's profile and could determine based on the IP address that the Chase Kingsley who's advertising his rugged good looks and the fact that he's a cop on the site is based in Swarthmore, a suburb of Philadelphia, and not, as it turns out, here in Hampton Cove."

"So it's not Chase?" Dooley asked.

"No, it's not. He's telling the truth. And so, incidentally, are my dad and Uncle Alec. Uncle Alec's search history only lists variations of the criminal he's been looking for, and my dad doesn't even have much of a search history. In fact he only looked at two profiles, and one of those is Gran."

"Gran is on the site?" I asked.

"Of course she is. And so is Scarlett, by the way."

"Why doesn't that surprise me?"

"What was the other profile Tex looked at?" asked Dooley.

Odelia smiled. "Mom's."

"Your mom is on Valina Fawn!" cried Dooley.

"A fact she conveniently forgot to mention," Odelia pointed out.

Well, looked as if all the men in our family were officially in the clear.

"So that's why you agreed to do the interview, and sit through that guy jabbering on about all of that nerdy stuff," I said.

Odelia nodded. "I simply had to know. And this seemed like the only way to find out. These sites are notoriously protective of that kind of information, but now that they've been so badly hit, they're anxious for positive publicity. And so I promised to give them a positive write-up..."

"In exchange for some information on Chase."

"We heard a big argument between Valina and Norwell," said Dooley. "Max says they're like rats on a ship, though they didn't seem eager to mate and produce half a billion offspring in the next three years."

Odelia laughed. "Yeah, I already had the impression they weren't as matey as they made out to be."

"Norwell says he's lawyering up," I said. "So they might get even less matey now."

"Understandable. Norwell left a great career and relocated his family to get involved with Valina Fawn. If the site goes bust, it's his reputation and his future on the line. So he'll want to distance himself as much as he can, and make sure his future employers know he's not to blame for the hack."

"Do you think there's negligence involved?" I asked.

"Hard to say. And of course they'd never admit it. But if people are going to start suing them, the truth might come out eventually. And it wouldn't surprise me if they didn't take a few shortcuts when they built that site. Shortcuts that left a lot of people's private details very vulnerable indeed."

That evening, I was happy to note that things were back to normal at Casa Kingsley. The couple were newly conciliated, and so were Tex and Marge, and even Uncle Alec and Charlene. Much to Gran's disappointment, all three men had proved absolutely blameless, and the love light shone bright once again.

Odelia was looking at a site dispensing advice to expecting moms, and keeping Chase abreast of her findings.

"Did you know that your boobs can grow up to two cup sizes?" she said.

Chase's eyebrows shot up. "Two cup sizes? Well how about that?"

"Some people seem to think that breastfeeding is a big no-no," she continued assimilating Dr. Google. "They say you should bottle-feed babies as much as possible."

"And why is that?" asked Chase, who was checking CNN on his phone.

"For one thing it might play havoc on your breasts. They might never be perky again."

"I don't mind if you don't mind," said Chase. He gave his wife a grin. "I like your boobies in any shape or size they come in, babe."

"The other reason is that some people seem to think that breast milk is bad for babies."

Chase frowned at this. "So the human species have been

doing it all wrong for the past couple of million years? Who wrote this nonsense?"

"Um... One Marjorie Bricks from Massachusetts. She says she's a licensed nurse."

"Well, you can tell Marjorie Bricks that she can take her advice and—"

"Chase! There's kids around," said Odelia with a quick glance to me and Dooley, who were listening with rapt attention.

"Oh, right," said Chase, and patted our heads distractedly.

Harriet and Brutus now strode in through the pet flap, looking a little listless, I thought. Unfortunately their contretemps hadn't been rectified by Odelia's findings. And so when Harriet hopped up onto the couch, miscalculated her approach shot and fell off again, instead of assisting his lady love, Brutus merely stood by and watched, a baleful look in his eye.

"Oh, lemon drop," said Harriet. "Don't be like that."

"Like what?" Brutus grunted.

"Like a big fat grump!"

"I'll stop being a big fat grump when you stop cheating on me with a bird," Brutus rejoined.

"I'm not cheating on you with anyone!"

Brutus now hopped up onto the couch and after having circled his spot thrice, as one does, finally lay down, still looking out of sorts. "I'll believe that when I see it," he grumbled.

"Max, say something!" said Harriet.

"What do you want me to say?" I asked.

"Tell Brutus he's the only one for me. And that no one will ever come between us, least of all some silly bird!"

Brutus seemed mollified by Harriet's pleas. After all, how could he not? It's not every day that someone pleads with you to believe in the purity of their intentions.

"All right," Brutus said finally. "I believe you."

"Oh, thank you, Pookie," said Harriet.

Brutus smiled. "I'm sorry," he said, "if I was being a big grump."

"That's okay," said Harriet. "You're my big grump."

"Oh, little monkey."

"Oh, snuggle bunny."

"Oh, sparky star."

"Oh, God," I moaned.

Just then, there was a strange sound at the window, and when we looked over, we saw that a bird was tapping against the pane with its beak. And when I looked closer, I saw that it was actually Jack the sparrow. When he saw that he finally had our attention, he drew himself up to his full height—which was negligible I must say—and started declamating loudly, "Harriet, queen of my heart. I've written a poem especially for you!" And before we could stop him, he cleared his throat, affected a strangely bleating diction, and trilled,

"Harriet, I'll marry it!

Harriet, I'll love it!

Harriet, I'll always be true!

Harriet, don't make me blue!"

At the conclusion of this expression of his immortal soul, Jack took a bow.

Brutus turned to Harriet, eyes burning with righteous fury, then hopped down from the couch and strode off on a huff without another word, though his rigid shoulders and unnaturally still tail spoke volumes.

"Pookie!" Harriet cried.

But Pookie was gone.

CHAPTER 8

It had already been a long day for Valina, and judging from the pile of work she still had on her desk, the day was about to turn into night with not a hope of a respite. Of course when you run your own business you can't expect to keep regular hours, but this was getting ridiculous.

She hadn't eaten a decent meal in days, practically hadn't seen her own bed in just as long, and in spite of all her efforts, the site was still in as precarious a position as when this whole disaster had struck.

She'd always had a soft spot for programmers, website designers and all manner of geek or nerd, but ever since her site was hacked, she hated the species with a vengeance. She imagined some army of nerds sitting in a basement somewhere thinking up ways and means of destroying other people's livelihood. It was digital vandalism, pure and simple, and if she could drag those shits through their monitor and skin them alive, she would.

She now settled back in her chair and rubbed her tired eyes. She'd managed to convince Norwell to stick with her, and the man had pulled off no mean feat by securing the site and plugging any hole that had made them vulnerable in the first place. Now all she had to do was convince people that this had been just a slight hiccup and that soon things would all go back to normal.

Oh, heck. Who was she kidding? Things would never go back to normal. It's one thing for a single person to have their private information leaked, but quite another for a happily married husband suddenly to see his name associated with a dating site. Judging from the avalanche of online abuse the site had suffered in the last twelve hours, a lot of people were very upset with her right now.

Then again, if you're going to cheat on your spouse, why not have the guts to come out into the open and admit to it? Why blame the middleman—or middlewoman, as in this case? She was, after all, simply a conduit for these people's adulterous ways.

And as she tried to focus on the letters on her laptop screen, which all seemed to dance and do the boogie-woogie, she suddenly thought she heard a sound coming from the big office next to her own corner office.

"Hello!" she called out. "Who's there?"

Probably a cleaner. Or someone having forgotten their wallet or phone.

But when she focused and listened some more, she didn't hear anything, and soon was immersed in the email she was writing once more. She wanted to shoot this one off now, so everyone would receive it in the morning when they arrived for work. It was one of those missives from the big brass that people tend to write at a time of crisis. Rallying the troops, and hoping they won't leave what they perceive as a sinking ship.

And as she was trying to think up a nice turn of phrase that wouldn't sound as harsh as 'disaster,' suddenly she thought she heard the sound of a footfall. And when she looked up, at first she couldn't really see anything, what with her eyesight having suffered from the strain of looking at a laptop screen for hours on end.

But when she finally focused, she saw that a black-clad person had materialized in her office. The figure was simply standing there, staring at her for some reason.

"Yes?" she said, frowning. "What do you want?"

But even as she spoke the words, the person shifted, and she saw they were holding what looked like a bow in their hands. Then the bow was raised, and before she fully realized what she was seeing, there was a swooshing sound, then a *thwack!* and pain suddenly bloomed in her chest.

She gasped to draw breath, but it was to no avail.

Her lungs refused to comply with such a simple demand.

Perhaps it was because her heart had already stopped beating.

CHAPTER 9

I really hadn't thought we'd be back at the offices of Valina Fawn so quickly. Only whereas yesterday we were there for an exclusive interview with the site's principals, today we were there in a completely different capacity. One that wasn't quite as pleasant.

"It's strange, isn't it, Max?" said Dooley when we found ourselves staring up at the not-quite-alive Valina. "Yesterday she was alive, and now she's dead. How did that happen?"

"That's for Chase and Odelia to find out," I said as I studied the body more closely.

"No, but I mean, we only saw her yesterday, and now she's gone. It makes you think."

"Yes, it most certainly does. For instance, who might have done this to her?"

"I was thinking more about life and death and that kind of stuff," said my friend the philosopher. "I mean, the human body is quite fragile, isn't it? That it only takes a minor incident like this to make it stop functioning at full capacity?"

"Not just the human body, Dooley. Any body will stop functioning when you shoot an arrow through its heart."

"But why, Max? Shouldn't the heart be made of sterner stuff? It's just a little bit of metal, after all. No reason why that should stop the heart from working properly."

"Well, it would appear it did the trick in this case," I said.

"Who found her?" asked Chase to one of the officers on the scene.

"Cleaner, sir. Came in here around seven to clean the office and called it in. Said she had a lot of trouble convincing the dispatcher that she was reporting an actual crime."

"What do you mean?"

"Dispatcher seemed to think she was playing a practical joke on her. Said that wasting police time is a punishable offense and if she didn't get off the phone she'd sue her."

Chase shared a look of annoyance with Odelia, then nodded. "I'll take care of it."

Abe Cornwall, the county coroner, was standing over the body, closely inspecting the wound. Then he stretched, planting his fists in his back and wincing. There was a slight creaking sound as his vertebrae resumed their regular working position. "It's the climate," he explained without invitation. "I need to go off someplace warm. Florida would be nice. Work miracles for my joints."

"So what do we have, Abe?" asked Chase, showing an appalling lack of interest in Abe's joints or his desire for warmer climes.

"Well, she's dead, all right," said Abe. "Shot through the heart with an arrow, I would say. Does the trick every time."

"What's with the toy?" asked Chase, referring to the small plush bear sitting in the dead woman's lap.

"That's Cupid," said Odelia. "It's Valina Fawn's logo. She uses it on everything. On the site, promotional materials, social media..."

The dead dating site leader sat bolt upright in her chair,

eyes open and staring into space. The arrow had passed right through her, and had lodged itself in the chair, keeping her pinned in her final position.

"She must have been facing her attacker, wouldn't you say?" asked Odelia.

"Yeah, I wonder what she saw," Chase murmured. He glanced around. "No cameras, unfortunately, and nothing to tell us who her attacker might have been."

"When did she die?" asked Odelia.

"I'd say between midnight and two o'clock," said Abe, "but don't pin me down on it," he added with a grin. His feeble attempt at humor clearly wasn't appreciated, and he proceeded to give instructions to the crime scene technicians processing the office.

The same officer from before now walked up holding a plastic evidence bag. It contained a smartphone. "Miss Fawn's phone, sir," he said. "Last call she received was from a Norwell Kulhanek. This would have been at twelve-thirty. Call was refused. Oh, and Mr. Kulhanek's key card was used to access the building at one-fifteen. He was the last person to enter the building. We don't know when he left—exits aren't logged."

"And before then? Who was the last person to enter?"

The officer produced what looked like a log. "Last person to enter was Miss Fawn herself, at six o'clock last night. And then the first entry after Mr. Kulhanek is the cleaner using her own key card. She was logged in at six forty-five this morning."

"Interesting," said Chase. "Thanks, Randal. Good job."

"Thanks, sir," said the young officer, looking pleased as punch.

"We better have a chat with our Mr. Kulhanek," said Chase.

"I interviewed him yesterday," said Odelia. "He and Valina

presented a united front, but later on Max and Dooley heard them arguing about who was responsible for the hack. He threatened to sue."

"You have an address for this Kulhanek character?"

But if Odelia did have an address for the man, she didn't need to dig it out, for at that moment the guy suddenly materialized in the office. And as he stood there, rooted to the spot, and staring at the body of his business partner, he uttered a strangled sort of cry.

Chase cursed under his breath. "What part of 'seal off the place' is so hard to understand?" he said, and walked out with long-legged stride to rectify the situation.

Odelia was left to deal with Norwell, who was staggering slightly. She escorted him out of the office and then into one of the empty offices to the side of the big open-office space that was the main hub of all the activity.

"I heard that something had happened," Norwell explained as he absentmindedly wiped his brow with the back of his hand, "but I didn't... I never..." He looked up at Odelia. "Is she..."

Odelia nodded. "I'm afraid so."

"But how? When? Who?"

"That's what we're trying to find out."

"But... I saw her just yesterday. She was fine."

"See?" said Dooley. "He's also surprised, Max."

"I think we're all surprised, Dooley. It's a natural reaction."

"I talked to her. We discussed strategies. Trying to get us out of this situation."

"Is it true that you threatened to sue?" asked Odelia. "Claiming this whole business was bad for your reputation?"

The man stared at her for a moment, then said, "Yes, well, in the heat of the moment I probably said a few things I shouldn't have said. But then when we talked things through,

I decided to stick around and help her deal with the fallout. Make the site bulletproof. Valina had a strategy in place. She wanted to use this hack as an opportunity to sell Valina Fawn as the best-protected, safest dating site on the market. She was great at that sort of thing."

"The thing is, Mr. Kulhanek," said Odelia, "that your key card was used to access the building last night. In fact you were the last person to enter the office. According to the log this was at one-fifteen."

Silence reigned for a few minutes, while Norwell processed this information. "I don't get it," he said. "You're saying I was here last night?"

Odelia simply stared at him. She wasn't as good at this as Chase, but good enough to make Norwell blanch.

"But I wasn't," he finally blurted out. "I was home at that time. My wife—Emma will tell you. I was up until two, working out the kinks and trying to come up with a new design for the site infrastructure. We were going for a complete redesign. Rebuild the whole thing from the ground up. The original programmer who designed the current iteration left last year, and honestly when I came on board and saw what a mess he made of things, I was frankly appalled. Spaghetti code, we call it: you start with something, and you just keep on building and adding stuff, and soon the whole thing gets completely out of hand. But when I came on board initially Valina didn't want to go for a full redesign, which was going to take time and was going to run into money. I pushed hard for it, and she finally realized with the hack that I was right all along: that spaghetti code had left the site vulnerable, with holes like Swiss cheese."

Chase entered the office and closed the glass door behind him. "Can I see your key card, please, sir?" he asked immediately.

"I—I'm afraid I don't have it anymore," said Norwell,

turning a hunted look at Chase now. "I tried to enter the building just now and discovered that I seem to have lost it."

"You lost it," said Chase in a flat tone that didn't conceal his disbelief.

"Yes! I'm telling you it wasn't in my wallet when I arrived this morning. The security guy had to buzz me in."

Chase studied the man's face. Norwell was sweating now, I saw, and looking from Chase to Odelia. It didn't help that it was particularly hot in the office, and the atmosphere was muggy and uncomfortable.

"When was the last time you saw that card?" asked Chase finally.

"Well, yesterday morning, when I arrived for work."

"You didn't see it after you entered the building yesterday?"

"No—you don't pay attention to something like that, do you? Only when you need it."

"And the only time you need that card is to gain access to the building?"

"Yes. I know that in other places they use their key cards for all kinds of stuff, even to get the coffee machine working or go the bathroom, but not here. It's strictly an access card to get into the building. Which maybe," he said with a thoughtful frown, "is something we should look at. Restrict access to specific areas like the server room."

He seemed to have forgotten already that his business partner had been brutally murdered last night, his programmer mind turning to problems that needed solving.

I could tell that he was probably a great software engineer, but without Valina Fawn, the company was likely destined for the scrapheap of history now.

"One other matter, Mr. Kulhanek," said Chase. "Did you call Valina last night?"

"Yes. Yes, I did."

"What did you talk about?"

"I—well, she didn't pick up, actually."

"Why did you call her?"

"Well, to discuss the redesign, of course. She'd told me she wanted me to get started immediately. Make sure that we had something we could promise our clients. Though of course it was going to take weeks, maybe even months. I called to bounce off some ideas."

"Were you upset when she didn't pick up?"

"Not really. I figured she was probably busy. Or asleep. It was pretty late when I called. I'd been working, you see, and when I'm busy I tend to lose track of time."

"So you didn't jump into your car and drive to the office to talk things through with her in person when you couldn't reach her on the phone?" asked Chase.

"No! What is this? You're not accusing me of..." He pushed his glasses back up his sweaty nose. "I just figured we'd talk in the morning. She had a conference call scheduled with some of our investors, and wanted to be ready to give them some good news to counter all the bad publicity the site has been getting. We've been hemorrhaging customers, as you can imagine, and she wanted to stop the bleed as soon as possible."

Chase eyed the man closely, and let the silence stretch on for a few minutes, then finally nodded and said, "Please keep yourself available for further interviews, sir."

"I-I didn't kill her, if that's what you're suggesting."

"I'm not suggesting anything, Mr. Kulhanek."

"Okay, well... that-that's fine, I guess. So um... can I go now?"

"For now," Chase allowed tersely, and we watched the programmer walk out.

"So what do you think?" asked Chase the moment the man was gone.

"He sounded honest enough," Odelia determined.

"So if he's to be believed someone stole his key card yesterday, then used it last night to gain access to the building and to murder Valina Fawn?"

"Whoever it was must have known that Valina was going to work late."

"And must have had access to Norwell at some point yesterday."

"And must be able to handle bow and arrow with some proficiency."

"I wouldn't say some—I'd say a high degree of proficiency. That was a crack shot, babe. Straight through the heart at the first try. No other marks on the woman's body."

"From what distance does Abe think the arrow was shot?"

"Too soon to tell, I'm afraid," said Chase. "Why?"

"The further away the killer was standing, the better his aim."

Chase nodded. "I agree. So we're probably looking at a member of the Brookwell Archery Club for our killer."

"Is Norwell Kulhanek a member?"

"Wouldn't surprise me if he is."

"So you still think..."

"I wouldn't discount him. You said it yourself last night. The guy left a lucrative career to come to Hampton Cove and become a partner in Valina Fawn. His wife had to change careers, his kids had to change schools... We're talking a major shift in lifestyle here. And all of a sudden disaster strikes in the form of this hack. He blames Valina, they argue, he threatens to sue for reputational damages, she tries to mollify him by promising a complete site overhaul, spouting some soundbites about using this as an opportunity but of course he knows better. Knows it might spell the end of a promising career."

"So he uses his own key card to enter the office and shoot her?"

Chase grimaced. "You saw him. The guy is a nervous wreck. He wasn't thinking straight."

"Still. There are less conspicuous ways to kill a person. And whoever killed Valina added that plush Cupid to make it clear he was targeting both her and her site."

"So a disgruntled customer?"

"Or a disgruntled spouse."

CHAPTER 10

Valina's personal assistant Meghan Fray was the next person being led into our makeshift interview room. She was a raven-haired woman in her mid-twenties with remarkable sea-green eyes and wearing the same kind of business suit her boss favored. She was crisp to the point of bluntness, and far from being shocked by the murder of her employer seemed more annoyed by it, as if Valina's death had messed up her plans.

"Valina was under a lot of pressure, as you can imagine," said Meghan. "We all were, actually. You wouldn't believe the phone calls we've been getting, and the emails. People even showed up at the office, demanding we pay them back their membership fees, or threatening with lawsuits. It's been a very difficult time."

"Anyone in particular stick out?" asked Chase.

Meghan smoothed the hem of her skirt. "Well... one person did seem more determined to talk with Valina. We all tried to shield her as much as possible from all the abuse, of course, but this woman wouldn't take no for an answer. And since she's in a position to create a lot of trouble for us,

Valina finally decided to take her call. She later told me it was one of the worst five minutes of her life. The woman was absolutely furious, and demanded access to her partner's private information—information that luckily wasn't part of the leak. Things like the profiles he looked at, times he swiped right, dates set up. That kind of thing. Lucky for us the guy was in the clear. Had never once swiped right."

Odelia frowned. "What is the name of this woman?"

"Um... Charlene Butterwick," said Meghan. "The Mayor of Hampton Cove?"

Odelia and Chase both looked appropriately surprised by this piece of news. "Charlene Butterwick caused Valina to experience the worst five minutes of her life?" asked Odelia.

"That's what she said. Mayor Butterwick has the power to close us down, you see. Or at least that's what Valina said. And also, her partner is a cop or some... thing..." Her voice trailed off as she stared at Chase, then grimaced. "He's your boss, isn't he?"

Chase nodded.

"Oh, God."

"He's a cop, Miss Fray. Not an ax murderer," said Chase dryly.

"He also happens to be my uncle," said Odelia, "and I can assure you he's a great guy."

But Meghan didn't look convinced. What she was convinced of was that she'd just made a very serious faux pas. "Look, we're all on edge here. Valina more than the rest of us. Her business was on the line, and she worked around the clock to make things right. And now this." She shook her head, and I could see the lines on her forehead. She might not show it, but she was indeed affected by her boss's murder.

"Is there anyone else you can think of who might have done this?" asked Odelia gently.

"Apart from the Mayor and the Chief of Police?" Chase added for good measure.

Meghan's eyelid twitched. The woman was feeling the strain. "I can think of a couple of hundred people who might have done this. Or even a thousand. You can't imagine how angry people are, detective. You should see some of the emails we've received."

"On another note," said Chase, "Norwell Kulhanek claims his key card was stolen yesterday. Do you have any idea who might be responsible? Maybe something you saw or overheard?"

Meghan thought for a moment, then shook her head. "No, I'm sorry. This is the first I've heard of Norwell's key card going missing. Are you sure he hasn't simply misplaced it? The man is notoriously distracted when it comes to practical things. He once walked into a meeting with Chinese investors wearing bathroom slippers. He'd left the house wearing them, walked into the office, and into the meeting, and never once noticed."

And as Chase wrote down his email address, so Meghan could send him those nasty emails Valina had been getting, the PA looked down at Odelia's belly and smiled. "Congratulations," she said. "How many months?"

"Sixteen weeks," said Odelia. "That obvious, huh?"

"I've got three sisters with ten kids between them, so you can call me an expert."

"How about you? No plans in that department?"

"First I'll have to find the right guy."

"I'd imagine that shouldn't be a problem, working for a dating site."

"It's harder, actually. When you've worked for Valina Fawn for as long as I have, you kinda lose faith in mankind—especially the male segment, I should add." She quickly glanced over to Chase. "He's..."

"My husband, yes," said Odelia.

"You should count yourself lucky that you found one of the good guys. There's a lot of jerks out there, Mrs. Kingsley. And I do mean a lot."

❧

"So Charlene, huh?" said Chase as we got into his car. "Who would have thought?"

"She's a very passionate woman," said Odelia as she strapped herself in. "So when she found out that Uncle Alec was on Valina's site, she must have been furious."

"I hope she wasn't furious enough to drive over here last night and kill Valina."

"Uh-oh," said Odelia, and held up her phone for Chase's benefit, then for ours. It showed a video of Charlene in full archery regalia, holding up bow and arrow and smiling at the camera. As the video started playing, Charlene let rip an excellent shot, and as the camera zoomed in on the target, it showed the arrow, feathered vanes still quivering, as it pierced the center of the target. 'Perfect shot!' Charlene cried jubilantly.

"If Charlene killed Valina, do you think Uncle Alec will make the arrest?" asked Dooley.

"I doubt it," I said. "He'll probably let Chase do the honors. And besides, I very much doubt that Charlene is a killer."

"She could have been carried away by her emotions."

"Possible," I allowed. Though Charlene didn't strike me as a killer. She probably had other means at her disposal when dealing with a businessperson that provoked her ire. Like having them arrested for being in violation of some obscure council regulation.

"I'm still thinking about that Cupid doll, Max," said Dooley. "That wasn't very nice, was it?"

"Murder usually isn't nice, Dooley."

"No, but Cupid is supposed to fire an arrow through the heart of the people he's trying to link, isn't he? Only here he shot a real arrow, and instead of linking Valina in love, it killed her. It just makes you sit up and think, doesn't it?"

"It certainly made Valina sit up and think."

"As if the killer was trying to send a message."

"Yes, that seems to be very obvious."

"The message that love kills, Max."

"I don't know if that's what the killer was going for, exactly."

"No, but he was. This person who killed Valina, he was probably in love with her, only she turned him down and this is why he killed her. Unrequited love, Max. It's no laughing matter."

"Who's laughing, Dooley?"

He gave me a puzzled look. But before he could respond, Chase was parking his car in front of Town Hall, and moments later we were strolling in, determined to find out how Charlene had given Valina such a fright.

We found Charlene seated behind her mayoral desk, busy doing mayoral things and looking very mayoral indeed. Behind her, instead of a portrait of herself, a large map of Hampton Cove hung, and across from her, a big landscape portraying that same Hampton Cove, only presumably in some day of old, since I could see horse-drawn carriages, which isn't something you see in the streets nowadays.

She rose when we entered the office and gestured to two intricately carved wooden chairs in front of her desk. "Take a seat. What can I get you? Tea? Coffee? You're here about that dreadful business with Valina, I presume? How can I help you?" She then crossed her fingers and looked at us intently, ready to be of assistance.

"The thing is, Charlene," said Odelia, "that you called Valina yesterday, and made some threatening noises, apparently. So threatening, in fact, that you scared the living daylights out of her."

Instead of looking rueful, Charlene actually broke into laughter. "I did! Yes, you're absolutely right. I called her and gave her a good verbal beating, I'm afraid. Of course at the time I was feeling a little overwrought." She held up her hands. "Now I know what they say. Never pick up the phone in anger. Count to ten and take a deep breath. But I must say I didn't feel like counting to ten, or taking a deep breath. I felt like going in there, guns blazing, and letting her have it, double-barreled. And yes, I probably shouldn't have done that, and in hindsight I'm sorry I did, but what's done is done. And if you must know, what she told me took the sting out of the whole thing, and I felt much, much calmer."

"She told you that Alec never swiped right, never went out on a date, and was only interested in looking at profiles of women answering to the description of this so-called Black Widow," said Odelia.

"That's exactly what she said. And that's exactly what I needed to hear. So I apologized, told her I still thought it was a rotten thing to do to expose her clients like that, and hoped she'd fix her site so it wouldn't happen again, and she promised me she would and that was that."

"So you didn't go down there last night and shoot an arrow through her heart?" asked Chase.

Charlene's eyebrows rose. "Oh, my God! How can you even ask me that!" Then she closed her eyes and made a waving gesture with her hands. "I'm sorry. Of course you have to ask me that. After that phone call..." She opened her eyes again and placed her hands flat on her desk. "I did not go down to the offices of Valina Fawn last night, and I did not shoot Valina through the heart with an arrow. You happy now? Are we good?"

"It's not a question of me being happy or unhappy, Charlene," Chase grunted, looking distinctly unhappy, I would have said, "but of asking the kinds of routine questions we always ask under these circumstances. When we talked to Valina's PA she told us that your call was responsible for the worst five minutes in Valina's life. And then of course there's this." He nodded to Odelia, who placed her phone on the desk and played that video.

Charlene watched it dispassionately. "I'd completely forgotten about that, actually," she murmured. "When was this?" She frowned at the screen. "Oh, that's right."

"Where was this taken?" asked Odelia.

"You know where it was taken, Odelia," said Charlene with a touch of stiffness.

"Brookwell," said Odelia.

Charlene nodded and leaned back in her chair, then gazed out through her window at the scudding gray clouds. "Before I met your uncle, I was a single woman for a long time. A widow, actually. I met Jim at Brookwell, and for a while we were the club's top archers. Won all the competitions, had a great time. We got married a year after we met, and I was happy—actually happy that I'd found the great love of my life. Until one of the other club members told me that she'd seen Jim kissing a girl in the dressing rooms late one night. It soon transpired that Jim hadn't just kissed this one girl, but a whole slew of girls. Turned out that he had quite a reputation at the club as a ladies' man, though I would have used a different word for his behavior. When I confronted him he said it was just a dalliance—or dalliances, plural—and none of it meant anything. Not really. He seemed to expect I'd tolerate his behavior. As if sleeping with other women was what all men did. Jim died from heart failure before I had a chance to divorce him, but I would have—in a flash."

"My God," Odelia said.

"It took me a long time to get over the betrayal, and when I met your uncle it took me an even longer time to accept that not all men are like Jim. That there actually are some decent men out there. So naturally when I discovered that Alec's name was on that list..."

"It brought back your ex-husband's betrayal."

Charlene nodded.

"What about Brookwell?"

"The moment I found out about Jim's affair, I quit the club and have never set foot back there again. Too many bad memories connected with that place now. Good memories, too, of course, as you can probably tell from that video, but unfortunately the bad ones seem to have a habit of canceling out the good ones."

"Do you still have a bow lying around, Charlene?" asked Chase.

Charlene shot him an intent look, then finally shook her head. "I burned it. All of it."

CHAPTER 11

The Brookwell Archery Club is located on what had once been a farmer's field but where now a clubhouse had been erected and several lanes where club members could practice their art. Carlotta Brook, along with her husband Dennis, was on hand to answer a few questions about the club, and even though they didn't look overly concerned, it was obvious from the way Dennis kept a steady eye on Chase—not unlike the eye he kept on his target when firing off another arrow from his quiver—he wasn't completely at ease.

Then again, when the police drop by asking a lot of questions in connection to a murder inquiry, it takes a strong soul not to be affected. Even innocent people tend to crack under the strain when seated across from Chase when he's got his cop's cap firmly lodged on his cranium.

"So, Dennis. I couldn't help but notice that your name was on the Valina Fawn site," said Chase, opening the interview with a shot across the bow.

"Yes," said Dennis, shooting a quick glance at his wife. "Yes, it was."

Carlotta had turned her head away and was staring icily in the opposite direction.

We were seated in the clubroom, where usually a fun and frolicking atmosphere prevails, but which was now completely devoid of club members.

"Though I'd like to go on record and say that I never cheated on Carlotta. Not even once. Sorry, what did you say, darling?"

Carlotta had produced a sort of disparaging snort, but otherwise kept mum.

"No, but what I mean to say, I never once went out with anyone. I never even swept up, or down, or whatever it is you do on these sites."

"Swipe right if it's a match, I believe," said Chase.

"Yes. Yes, of course. Swipe right. Well, I never did. I only swiped left."

Carlotta turned back to her husband, looking furious. "You told me you never swiped at all! That the only reason you were on the site in the first place was to see what Jaymie was up to!"

"Jaymie?" asked Odelia.

"Our daughter," said Dennis, nervously licking his lips. "She told us she was on the site, and so I created a profile just to see what it was all about."

"To spy on your daughter, you mean," said Chase.

"No! Absolutely not. Just... well, you know. Keep up, I guess." He smiled an obsequious smile that didn't quite meet his eyes. In fact he had a sort of hunted look on his face that reminded me of certain species of dogs when they've been bad and are locked up in their kennel for the night, so they can have a good long think about their appalling behavior.

"Do you think Dennis was locked up in the doghouse last night, Max?" asked Dooley, proving he was on the same page.

"It wouldn't surprise me," I said as I took in the man's

furtive behavior. He even looked a little unkempt, I thought. As if he had slept in these same clothes.

"Look, darling, I never meant for you to find out—I mean it wasn't my intention for you to..." His voice trailed off, and he slumped a little more in his seat.

"What can you tell us about your movements last night?" asked Chase, deciding to put the guy out of his misery. "Let's say between midnight and two o'clock this morning?"

"I was home," said Carlotta. "Fast asleep at that time as usual. Early to bed, early to rise has been my motto ever since I was a professional archer."

"And you, sir?" asked Odelia.

"Me?" Dennis said in a small voice. "Well... home, of course."

"You weren't together?" asked Chase.

"If you really must know, Dennis slept on the couch last night," said Carlotta, with a seething glance at her errant spouse. "And if it's up to me, he'd better get used to it."

"But, darling, with my bad back..."

"You should have thought of that before you started fooling around with your whores!" Carlotta spat.

"But I never... I mean, I didn't even... Oh, darling—how can you be so cruel!"

"Cruel! You're the one being cruel, Dennis. And on the evening of our wedding anniversary, too!" She turned to Chase and Odelia. "We were going to organize a big party here at the club for our fifteenth wedding anniversary, but of course that's all off now."

"Caterers have been booked," Dennis murmured, looking in the dumps, "a live band is going to play—the Hootenannies—I've got the hippest DJ of the moment booked for the night—DJ Carl Quick— invitations have been sent—two hundred of them..." He sighed, and chanced a quick glance to his wife, but her implacable expression spoke volumes.

"So no one can actually vouch for your whereabouts last night?" asked Chase.

"Unless I crawled down through the window, Dennis would have noticed if I left the house. And I would have noticed if he crept out during the night, since the garage is right underneath the bedroom. But why would he sneak out to murder Valina? She gave him everything he needed. An unlimited supply of backstabbing, home-wrecking *whores*!"

"Honey, please!" Dennis pleaded. "What will people think!"

"They'll think you're dog excrement, Dennis, and they'd be thinking correctly."

"Darling!"

"Spare me the phony tears," said Carlotta, holding up her hand and turning away again.

"Did any of you drop by Valina Fawn at any point yesterday?" asked Chase.

Carlotta frowned. "Why would I want to go near the woman? And to think she was a member of the same book club and never even hinted that she'd lured my husband to his doom. Talk about duplicitous."

"You, Dennis?" asked Chase.

"No, I certainly didn't go anywhere near the place yesterday—or any other day."

"Do you know Norwell Kulhanek well?"

"Isn't he Emma's husband?" asked Carlotta. And when Odelia nodded, she said, "I don't think I've ever met the man. Isn't he a computer programmer or something?"

"He's the lead programmer on the Valina Fawn site," said Odelia.

This seemed to come as a surprise to Carlotta. "So Emma and Valina..."

"Emma isn't involved in the site. At all," Odelia was quick to say.

"Oh. Well, at least there's that."

"I never met the man," Dennis muttered miserably when Chase gave him an inquisitive look. "And as far as I know, neither he or Emma are members here at the club."

There didn't seem to be a need to ask the Brooks if they could think of anyone who would want to harm Valina. It was obvious there were plenty of candidates to choose from.

"I'm going to need to list of all your members," said Chase now.

"Why is that?" asked Dennis.

"Because of the way she was murdered, of course," said Carlotta. "Haven't you been paying attention?"

"How..." Dennis began.

"She was shot with an arrow, Dennis! Straight through the heart. And if you ask me, the killer was much too kind. He should have shot her through the spleen. Very painful death—or so I'm told."

As we walked back to the car, Chase was studying the list Dennis had printed out in his office. He whistled when he spotted one particular name. "Adra Elfman," he said, "and if memory serves, I think I saw a Mr. Elfman on Valina's list of clients."

"There could be others," said Odelia as she opened the door so we could hop into the car. "We better cross-reference both lists. We may come across a few more surprises."

CHAPTER 12

"Carlotta Brook is an Olympic archer," said Odelia once we were en route. "She actually won Olympic gold in her discipline."

"All the more reason to put her on our list of suspects," Chase grunted as he checked the GPS display. "And by the looks of things her husband could be next."

"Yes, she seems to be very upset with Dennis at the moment."

"Upset! If looks could kill the man would already have died the most excruciating death. She said the killer was being kind. *I'm* being kind by not arresting her on the spot." He frowned. "Do you think I should have arrested her? Just to make sure she doesn't kill Dennis?"

"I really don't think Carlotta is a killer," said Odelia. "She's the only one who read *Tears in the Mud* from cover to cover and even supplied Mom with some apt questions to discuss in book club."

"Your point being?"

"That she's a deeply sensitive and romantic soul, who wouldn't hurt a fly."

"You can like a book and still be a vicious killer, babe. One doesn't exclude the other, as I think prison librarians will tell you."

"Do you think Carlotta killed Valina, Max?" asked Dooley.

"Too soon to tell," I said. "Though she certainly had motive and means. I don't know about that key card, though. Seems unlikely that she had access to Norwell yesterday. Though she and Emma are both members of Marge's book club, but unless Carlotta dropped by Emma's yesterday... No, Norwell spent all day at the office, and he took his key card with him. So that seems to be out of the question." I frowned. "This whole thing seems to revolve around that key card. Who had access to it and when?"

"He had it when he went to work in the morning, so whoever took it," said Dooley, "must have taken it at the office somehow."

"Which narrows down our list of suspects considerably."

Odelia, who'd been listening to our conversation, said, "It does, doesn't it? We better check in again with Norwell. Have him go through his day, from the moment he arrived until he went to bed. Whether he dropped by a shop, or the fitness club, or even took the dog for a walk. We need to know when the killer had the opportunity to get that key card."

"Unless Norwell is our guy," I said. "In which case it's pretty obvious how he did it."

"Yes, obvious, but not necessarily true," said Odelia.

She pored over the two lists now, the Brookwell member list and the Valina Fawn client list. "There are too many names here to do this on the fly," she finally admitted.

"I already sent both lists to one of my officers," said Chase. "They'll handle it."

We'd arrived at the cozy little home of the Elfmans, Adra and Gene. A nice apron of green with plenty of colorful flowers fronted the house, which was obviously well-kept. Chase parked his squad pickup and we all got out. Moments later we were sitting in a small but pleasantly furnished living room, Odelia and Chase sipping from cups of coffee, and Dooley and I being fed a piece of cold chicken that tasted quite delicious.

"I like being a detective, Max," said Dooley. "People are always so nice to us."

"That's because they don't want to go to prison," I said. Though we weren't always received in this way. Some people, when they opened the door and found a cop flashing a badge in their faces, slammed the door shut and made a run for it through the backdoor.

Of course both Adra and her husband Gene were probably not sprightly enough to try and shake off Chase when he was in full pursuit mode. Very rare is the criminal who can shake that man off once he gets going. Except Usain Bolt, maybe, who's no criminal.

"I take it you're not here to talk about book club?" asked Adra.

"Not exactly," said Odelia. "I don't know if you heard what happened to Valina?"

Adra's face crumpled. "Horrible news. The mailman told us this morning."

"Terrible business," Gene agreed with his wife.

Both of them were seated in matching armchairs, strategically positioned in front of a large television. For their guests the sofa offered satisfactory seating, and for me and Dooley there was always the carpet.

"I would have expected them to have a dog," said Dooley. "A small one, you know. Like a Yorkie or a Pekinese or even a Chihuahua."

"Some people don't like dogs," I said. "Or maybe they once had a dog and it died and now they don't want another."

"What do you think happened to the dog?" asked Dooley, as always fascinated by death in all its facets. "Do you think someone shot it through the heart like Valina?"

"I'd say chances of that are slim to nonexistent."

"I saw that you are a member of the Brookwell Archery Club, Ada?" asked Odelia.

"Yes, that's right. You didn't know? I used to shoot a lot when I was younger. Nowadays I rarely go anymore, though I keep renewing my membership, more for old time's sake than anything else, I suppose." She smiled a sweet smile at Odelia. "But I'm sure that's not the only reason you came here. You probably discovered that my Gene was on Valina's list. And now you're wondering if I went over there last night to kill the woman?"

"Well, the thought had crossed my mind," Odelia admitted.

"I never signed up for that thing," said Gene, who had a sort of crumpled look. Both his clothes, which appeared a little too large for him, and his skin, which had the same effect. "It was Lily who was responsible. She probably thought it was a good joke."

"Who's Lily?" asked Chase, who was taking notes.

"Our granddaughter," said Adra. "She's thirteen, and is into practical jokes. Last month she signed me up to fly to Mars and start populating a new colony. And now this month it's Gene who got it in the neck. Please don't read too much into it. It's her age, I guess."

Chase smiled. "So are you going to repopulate Mars, Mrs. Elfman?"

"I've raised three daughters. I would think I've done my share," the elderly lady laughed. "Besides, who wants to travel to some dead planet when we've got a perfectly nice one down here?"

"How about you, Mr. Elfman?" asked Odelia. "Have you ever swiped right?"

Gene frowned. "Swiped where?"

"Gene isn't into computers," said the man's wife. "Our eldest bought him a tablet last Christmas, and I have to say he tried his best, but in the end we simply gave it back."

"The internet is a dangerous place," Gene grumbled as he gave Chase an accusatory look, as if he held him personally responsible. "Full of crooks and cheats. My son-in-law got a message last week, telling him that he won something called bitcoin. The fool clicked on the message and now his phone has been hacked. He'll have to buy himself a new one."

"Our daughter wants us to try out this online banking thing," said Adra, "but I told her we better not. A friend of ours lost all of her savings when someone from the bank called. Or at least he told her he was from the bank. A very nice man, too. Ever so friendly. Turns out it was some kind of scam and she ended up transferring all of her savings to this man."

"Police won't do a damn thing," Gene grunted. "And the bank refuses to give her back the money, claiming it was her own damn fault for being so gullible in the first place."

"Harriet chatted with a United States Marine," said Dooley. "But it turns out it was Rufus instead. Rufus is a dog," he added for good measure. "A very nice sheepdog."

But of course Adra and Gene couldn't appreciate Dooley's contribution to the conversation, since they didn't speak our language.

"So," said Adra finally, patting her knees. "Are we still on for book club tonight?"

"Again?" asked Gene. "I thought you just had your book club meeting?"

"What with one thing and another, we never got to finish discussing *Tears in the Mud*," said Adra, "which is why Marge proposed a second meeting." She shot a look at Odelia. "Though now with Valina murdered, I guess we should probably postpone."

"I'll ask Mom," Odelia promised.

"Tell her to give me a call."

"Did you know," said Gene, scooting forward in his armchair, "that there are people out there who can spy on you through your computer? Take pictures, even? Just imagine for a moment, young man, that you're taking a shower and some person on the other side of the world decides to snap pictures of your willy? How about them apples, huh?"

I had the distinct impression that Gene could talk for hours about the dangers we all faced in this brave new internet world, but Chase and Odelia still had more witnesses to interview, so they decided to thank the couple for their time and be on their way.

Pity, I thought, since when Adra had opened the fridge I'd spotted another nice piece of chicken in there, just waiting for me and Dooley to sink our teeth into.

Then again, who knows what the next person had in store for us?

CHAPTER 13

Our final interview of the day—and I must admit I was glad for it, since I was starting to yearn for a nice long nap—was Emma Kulhanek. Chase and Odelia wanted to find out if her husband Norwell had indeed been home when he said he was, and the best way to find out was to go straight to the source of the man's marital bliss—as professed by both.

"Oh, yes, he was here," said Emma as soon as the question had been laid before her. "He arrived home late, but then he often does, and now with this big mess at the site he's got a ton of work to get through, as you can imagine."

"What time did he get home?" asked Odelia.

"Oh, around eight, I should say? I'd kept his dinner in the oven, and warmed it up as soon as he walked through the door. I kept him company and then he went upstairs and went straight back to work in his office. I'm afraid that when I went to bed he was still at it, slaving away at that site."

"When did you go to bed?"

"Late. I keep telling myself I'll turn in early, but I never seem to manage. I start watching something on TV and before I know it it's almost midnight."

"So you went to bed around midnight would you say?" Chase insisted.

"A little later," said Emma, looking sheepish. "Twelve-fifteen. Something like that."

"And your husband was still working in his office?"

"Yeah, I went in there for my goodnight kiss," said Emma, looking amused. "I don't understand. What's this all about?"

"You haven't heard?" asked Odelia.

"Heard what?"

"Valina was murdered last night."

Emma's eyes went wide, and her face took on a paler hue. "Oh, my God—murdered!"

"We thought you knew," said Chase.

"Didn't Norwell tell you?"

"No, he didn't. I haven't heard from him all day. He's been at the office, busy as usual, trying to build a new site for Valina." She looked dismayed now. "So all these questions… I thought it had to do with the hack, but you're looking for Valina's murderer?"

"Valina was killed between midnight and two o'clock last night," said Chase, "and your husband's key card was used to gain access to the building at one-fifteen. So we can safely assume that the murder was committed at that time."

Her eyes widened, fully aghast. "You're not seriously suggesting that Norwell…"

"He claims that someone took his key card," said Odelia. "He had it when he badged in yesterday morning, but this morning when he arrived he discovered it wasn't in his wallet, where he keeps it. So someone must have stolen it between the time he arrived for work yesterday and the time Valina was shot at one-fifteen last night."

"Shot? You mean like with a gun?"

"With bow and arrow," said Chase, studying Emma's face.

If a person could personify shock and dismay, Emma did a perfect job at it. She looked absolutely flabbergasted. "Oh, my God," she muttered, then frowned. "It can't have been Norwell," she finally said. "I'm a very light sleeper. In fact I always wake up when Norwell comes to bed. He's already told me to use earplugs but I can't wear them. My ears just start to itch and hurt when I do, even the hypoallergenic ones he got me from the pharmacy. So if he'd left the house at any time during the night I would have heard."

"You're sure about that?" asked Chase.

"Absolutely. I even wake up when the kids sneak downstairs for a glass of water. It's very annoying. Though Norwell says it's a good thing. He sleeps like a log, you see. You can fire off a cannon and he wouldn't wake up. If the house caught fire I'd be the one getting everyone out of bed and safely outside on the lawn waiting for the fire trucks to arrive."

"I'm a light sleeper, too," said Dooley.

"All cats are," I said. "We wake up from the least sound or movement."

"Emma should get herself a couple of cats. She'll feel right at home with them."

"What can you tell us about the relationship between your husband and Valina?" asked Chase, clearly not fully satisfied that Norwell hadn't somehow fooled us all.

"They were getting along fine, until this whole business with the hack started. Valina blamed Norwell, since he's in charge of programming, and he blamed her, since the site was designed before he came on board and he told her several times it wasn't up to snuff."

"Is it safe to say that they argued a lot?"

"Oh, absolutely. But that's only understandable. After all, we both gave up a lot to come here. We had a good life in San Francisco. I had a good teaching position, the kids loved their school and their friends, and Norwell was doing great."

"So why come here?" asked Odelia.

"The challenge of designing a site from scratch. The chance to become a partner. And of course I was born and raised in Hampton Cove. My family is here, and I'd always dreamed one day of moving back. Send the kids to the same school I went to. Be a teacher there. And so far it's worked out fine. Until the big hack drama happened." Her face fell. "And now of course this murder." She gave Chase an anxious look. "What's going to happen now? Are they going to close down Valina Fawn for good?"

"I don't know, Emma," said Chase. "That's not for the police to decide."

"But you have shut down the site, right? With the murder and everything?"

"No, the site is still up and running as far as I know," said Chase. "Though we have closed down parts of the office for the time being, since it's a crime scene."

"I understand," said Emma quietly. "Well, I guess we'll just have to wait and see." She looked up. "So do you have any suspects yet? People who could have taken Norwell's card?"

"It's still early days," said Chase. "Right now we're trying to interview as many people who can shed light on the case as possible." They both got up. "If there's anything else, just give us a call. Any time, day or night. Even the smallest detail might be important."

"Of course," said Emma. "Of course I will."

She waved us off, still wearing that slightly dazed and worried look on her face. And I didn't wonder why that was. Her husband was clearly Chase's prime suspect. And in spite of her protestations, I had a feeling Chase didn't give much credence to her story about waking up at the slightest sound. If a man is determined to go out and murder a person, he'll always find a way.

CHAPTER 14

That evening, much to everyone's surprise, Marge had decided to organize a book club meeting again. She felt that especially now, with everything that was going on, and with the death of Valina, it was important to get together and bask in the warmth of friendship and companionship. The last book shop meeting had ended in acrimony, with the clash between Lynnette and Emma, but tonight was all about healing and coming together.

"I still find it hard to believe that Valina is gone," said Adra, a copy of *Tears in the Mud* clasped firmly in her hand. "She was such a powerful force in the community, and I always loved her take on Marge's book choices."

"Well, I didn't," said Carlotta, who clearly hadn't yet dropped her intense dislike of the dating site boss. "I found her comments vapid and devoid of finesse. But then what can you expect from a woman who makes her money facilitating adultery?"

"Maybe we should adopt a more conciliatory tone," said Marge hastily, before things got out of hand again. "After all, Valina isn't here to defend herself anymore."

Carlotta didn't seem entirely convinced, but when the others all nodded their agreement, she wisely kept her tongue.

"I have to agree with Carlotta, though," said Lynnette Say. "I'm just glad that my Franco wasn't on Valina's site."

"That doesn't mean anything," said Carlotta. "He could have been using an alias."

Lynnette laughed a light tinkling laugh. "I know for a fact that Franco would never cheat on me. And that's because I've always made sure that he has no reason to."

Carlotta frowned. "What's that supposed to mean?"

Lynnette studied her perfectly manicured nails. "If a man doesn't get what he wants at home, of course he'll go looking for it elsewhere. If you want to keep your husband happy, you have to make an effort, and that's where most women go wrong. They get lazy, and then they come crying when they find out he's been out playing the field."

"So you actually have the gall to tell me it's my fault that Dennis was on Valina's list?"

Lynnette smiled a sweet smile. "I'm sure I wouldn't presume to know what makes your marriage work, Carlotta. I'm just telling you how I've succeeded in making mine work."

"Well, for your information I'm starting to think that I totally overreacted," said Carlotta. "Dennis may have signed himself up for the site, but he swears up and down that he was never unfaithful to me." She sighed. "And I'm inclined to believe him. Dennis may be many things but he's not a smooth operator. I think I'd know if he was lying to me."

"Same thing here," said Lynnette. "Men are so obvious, aren't they? Like sad little puppies when they don't get what they want. And then when you give it to them they get all overexcited and practically wet themselves. Not," she hastened to say, "that Franco has a problem in that department. He passed his recent prostate exam with flying colors."

"I'm glad that Gene hates technology so much," said Adra. "He wouldn't even know how to work a smartphone, let alone get in touch with other women that way."

"I can totally relate how so many people are completely devastated right now by the news that their significant other signed up for Valina's site," said Emma. "I was the victim of a cheating partner once and I can tell you that it hurts like the dickens."

"And that takes us right back to our topic for tonight," said Marge smoothly.

Carlotta frowned at her copy of *Tears in the Mud*. "Not exactly Dickens," she said.

"No, but I was thinking we could tackle Dickens next," said Marge. "Though I'm not sure yet which one. He has so many wonderful books to choose from."

"I thought we could do a Nora Roberts one," said Adra eagerly.

"It doesn't always have to be romance, Adra," said Lynnette sternly. "There are other genres to choose from, you know."

Adra's face fell. It was clear she preferred romance. "Nora writes mystery, too," she ventured hopefully.

"That's true," Marge agreed. "You know what I'll do? I'll draw up a list for you to choose from. And everyone is invited to nominate books for the list. How does that sound?"

"Excellent," said Charlene, who was nibbling from a cookie. She looked a little worn out, but then being mayor will do that to a person. It's a tough job at the best of times, and when dating sites get hacked and their CEOs murdered, it gets even worse. "You know, just for the record, I have to say I don't agree with what you just said, Lynnette."

"About romance, you mean?" asked Lynnette, raising a stunned eyebrow.

"No, about women being responsible for their husbands cheating on them."

"I don't think I phrased it exactly like that," said Lynnette with a light laugh.

"Yes, you did. And you really shouldn't blame women when their husbands turn out to be philandering you-know-whats. Mostly it's the men themselves that are up to no good. And unfortunately I can relate." She gave Emma a sad look. "And even though I blamed myself for a long time, I know now that it wasn't my fault. In fact it never was."

"Hear, hear," said Adra. "So about Nora. She writes in many wonderful genres. She writes mystery, romance, but also fantasy and even science fiction!"

"And her books are a damn sight better than that Dickens fellow," Carlotta murmured.

"Dickens is classic literature," said Odelia, coming to her mom's defense. "And you can't deny that he wrote some very… interesting books. Books that are still being read today."

"All right, fine," said Lynnette. "So let's put it to a vote. All in favor of Nora—"

"First the nominations, then the vote," said Marge, showing everyone who was boss. "There's an order to these things and it's important to respect it, otherwise it's chaos."

Just then, Gran walked in, saw that the meeting was in full swing, and immediately walked out again.

Gran isn't one for reading, I'm afraid, and in that sense she's an equal opportunities person: she dislikes Nora just as much as she dislikes Dickens or any other writer. And since book club occupied the living room, where the television is located, I could already tell she was in a bad mood, for next door, Chase was watching football with Tex and Alec.

"Now she knows how we feel," Dooley whispered.

"And how do we feel?" I asked, yawning widely.

"Not in control of the remote!"

CHAPTER 15

Vesta was indeed in a particularly foul mood. She didn't enjoy it when she couldn't occupy her space the way she liked. And most of all she didn't enjoy not being able to watch her favorite shows in peace and comfort. Of course she had a small television set in her bedroom, but the last thing she wanted was to sneak upstairs and hide away in her room like some punished teenager and watch TV. After all, what's the point of having a perfectly nice house with a perfectly nice TV when you can't even call the place your own!

So she set off for Odelia's place, knowing that at least there these so-called book club people wouldn't be infesting the place with their intellectual pastime. Only the moment she stalked in through the kitchen door, she found not only her son-in-law there, stretched out on the couch, but also Tex and even her son Alec. The three men were watching some football game on television.

"Oh, hey, Vesta," said Tex good-naturedly. "Wanna join us?"

"And watch grown men beat the crap out of each other?

No, thank you very much." And she made to leave again, vowing to drop by Scarlett's and hog her friend's TV instead.

"Oh, before you go," said Alec, "there's been a complaint. Well, a couple of complaints, actually."

"What complaint?" she asked, glancing to the TV where two colossuses had just collided. She winced, imagining the damage to the brain these people must endure.

"The cleaner at Valina Fawn who called in Valina's murder this morning. You told her not to waste valuable police time with her crank calls and hung up on her. Lucky for her she got Scarlett the second time around, who did the right thing and sent a patrol round."

"So? What's your point, exactly?" she asked tersely.

Alec took a deep breath. "My point, Ma, is that when you're a 911 dispatcher, you don't tell people reporting a crime to take a hike. You diligently follow protocol and take down their information and send a unit. Didn't you get the flow chart outlining the procedure?"

"Chucked it," she snapped. "Don't need no stinkin' flow charts telling me what to do. What am I? A nine-year-old? As if I can't distinguish between a crank call and the real thing."

"Well, obviously you got the wrong end of the stick this morning. So please, Ma, don't let it happen again? Or I'll be forced to take measures."

She narrowed her eyes at her one and only son. "What measures?"

"I'm afraid I'll have to let you go if it happens again."

She gaped at the man. "Let me go! Your sweet old mother! Have you no shame!"

"I'm sorry, Ma, but in the interest of public safety... You have to admit you dropped the ball there this morning."

"I did no such thing! On the contrary, I saved your people a lot of time and trouble looking into an unnecessary report by what was obviously some crazy person."

"That crazy person reported the murder of her boss," said Alec sternly.

She clamped her lips together. "Anything else you want to share with me?"

"There have been several complaints about your tone."

"My tone? What's wrong with my tone?"

"Apparently you sound very cranky."

"Cranky! I'm Miss Congeniality!"

"You told a woman to stop whining when she reported her car had been stolen."

"No one likes a crybaby," Vesta muttered darkly.

"And you told Rory Suds he was acting like a diva when he called in a holdup."

"Probably just a couple of his drug addict buddies unhappy with his merchandise."

Alec gave another weary sigh. "Just... be nice to people, will you? Make an effort?"

"I'm always nice to people. Just ask Tex. You can't wish for a nicer person than me."

But when Tex preferred to stay mum on the subject, and in doing so refused to endorse her view of herself, she made a sound of disgust and stalked out.

"Fine!" she said. "You don't have to spell it out. I know when I'm not welcome!"

"Vesta, don't be like that," said Chase, but she was already slamming the door.

Fifteen minutes later she was parking her daughter's aged red Peugeot in front of Scarlett's apartment building, and another five minutes later was sipping a hot cocoa on her friend's living room couch. "I mean, the gall of these people," she was saying. "It's not enough that I have to listen to these attention seekers all day, and spend my precious time cooped up inside a stinky old precinct, now they've got the nerve to file a complaint!"

"You gotta understand, hon," said Scarlett, who was drinking her usual black coffee, "that these people are under a lot of stress. Imagine having your house burgled, or suddenly staring at the business end of a big gun, wielded by an obviously unbalanced person high on crystal meth. The last thing you expect is to be called a diva or told to man up when you call in the cops. They want to be told that everything is gonna be all right. That help is on the way. That they can count on us to put an end to their nightmare."

Vesta frowned before herself, but had to admit Scarlett just might have a point.

"You know what your problem is, Vesta? You lack empathy."

"Are you kidding! I'm full of empathy! I'm empathy personified. What is empathy, exactly?"

Scarlett smiled. "Empathy is being able to put yourself in the other person's shoes. Seeing things from their perspective and responding accordingly. So when a person calls in a murder, you don't tell them to take a hike and stop wasting valuable police time. You try to imagine how *you* would feel if you came face to face with a dead body."

"I'd probably freak out a little," Vesta admitted. "And then I'd call the cops."

"And if the person on the other end told you to buzz off?"

"Then I'd probably drag them through the phone line and beat the living crap out of them." She frowned. "Okay, if you put it like that, maybe I did overreact a little."

"A little! You're probably the worst police dispatcher in history!"

"Oh, don't you start, too," she grumbled, trying to deflect blame, as was her habit. "Can I help it that I never received the proper training? That I was dumped into this job without so much as an instruction manual?"

"I was dumped into this job, and I'm doing all right."

"That's because you're a *nice* person," she growled, making it sound as if being nice was akin to being a mass murderer.

"You could be nice, if you wanted to be. It might take an effort at first, because you're not used to it, after spending your whole life being an obnoxious b—"

"Don't you say it! Don't you dare!"

"—busybody."

She glared at her friend for all of a minute, trying to decide whether to fly off the handle or not, but finally decided that maybe she had enough of that kind of behavior.

So finally she said, "You're right."

Scarlett blinked. "Excuse me?"

"I said you're right."

Scarlett's smile was something to behold. "Could you please repeat that, only this time I'll record it on my phone?"

"Don't be such a smart-ass," she said, then rested her chin on her hand. "I'm not a very nice person, am I?"

"No, you're not, but you are pretty funny."

"Funny!" she spat. "What does that even mean?"

"It means you always make me laugh, with your outrageousness."

"Fat lot of good that has ever done me," she muttered, staring before herself. "It's just... I don't suffer fools gladly, Scarlett. And there are a lot of fools out there. And I do mean a lot."

"I know," said Scarlett. "But maybe you shouldn't let them get to you."

"I'm simply too good for this world, that's my problem."

"Of course it is," said Scarlett with a grin.

"No, but it's true!" After a moment, she returned her friend's grin, and before long, both women shared a hearty laugh. "I don't know how you tolerate me," she finally said.

"Yeah, I ask myself that all the time," Scarlett returned.

Vesta gave her friend a light slap on the thigh, then both

friends settled in as Scarlett turned on the television, and moments later they were watching *The Good Wife*.

Vesta soon found herself spacing out, though, Alicia's exploits not as gripping as usual. Could it be that Scarlett was right? That she lacked empathy? It certainly was a novel concept that you needed to empathize with people. She usually bulldozed her way through life, and so far it had been a winning strategy. Now, though, she wasn't so sure.

Definitely something to explore.

CHAPTER 16

As Dooley and I got ready to go to cat choir, Harriet and Brutus decided to join us. They seemed to have patched things up, for they were once again on speaking terms.

"She's agreed to cancel her Pettr account," Brutus told me in confidence as we walked along. "And I've agreed to be more trusting going forward. After all, when you're in a relationship it's all about giving each other space, isn't it?" he added magnanimously.

"I suppose," I said, darting a quick glance to Harriet, who was walking next to Dooley, and telling him everything about her Pettr experience. Not that Dooley seemed to grasp the full gist of the Pettr concept, but that has never stopped Harriet before.

"I mean, you need to give them that space, you see. It shows how much you trust the other person. And after all, when there's no trust, what is there? Nothing, Max!"

"Uh-huh," I said, finding this conversation passing into Dear Abby territory a little too much for my personal taste. I'm not an agony aunt, and therefore not equipped to give advice to the lovelorn or even quarreling lovebirds like Brutus and Harriet.

"So I've decided not to check her Pettr account from now on."

"I thought you said she agreed to cancel her account?"

"That's what she said, but how do I know she isn't lying? But to show her how much I trust her, I'm not even going to check." He lowered his voice. "So could you do me a favor and find out?"

"Find out what?"

He frowned at me. "If she canceled her account, of course!"

"But I thought you said you were going to trust her? Give her space and all that?"

"And I am giving her space. But that doesn't mean you have to give her space."

"Really, Brutus? You want me to spy on Harriet for you? Is that what it's come to?"

"Just this once, buddy." He gave me a pained look. "I need to know. I'm going to go stir-crazy if I don't. So can you do me this one little favor? Just take a peek at her tablet for me?"

"Oh, all right," I said.

"Do it after you get back from cat choir. I've promised to take her into town, to the Hungry Pipe. I hear they've got quite the menu lined up for us tonight."

"They have?"

"Well, not for us, specifically. There's a council meeting tonight, and several council members have gotten into the habit of heading to the Hungry Pipe for a late dinner. And you know what those council members are like. After a lifetime in politics, their digestive systems are completely screwed up, so there'll be plenty of leftovers for us to snack on."

"Fine," I said, though I quite liked the idea of snacking on some tasty leftovers. Then again, Brutus was my friend, and it sounded as if he could really use a helping paw tonight. "I'll do it. But what if she hasn't canceled her account? Then what?"

"I-I don't know." He eyed me uncertainly. "What do you think I should do?"

"Let's not get ahead of ourselves. For all we know she has canceled her account."

"Of course she has," he said, relaxing. "Harriet wouldn't lie to me. I trust her."

Somehow, though, it didn't exactly sound as if he believed this himself.

As usual, cat choir was a pleasant enough affair. Shanille had a new song for us to try out. It was the theme from *Cats*, which is a musical about cats, apparently, and also a movie. I was fine with it, though some of our members weren't, since they felt that no human could accurately capture the essence of cathood and so we shouldn't dignify this Andrew Lloyd Webber, who was an Englishman to boot, by putting our not inconsiderate talent at his disposal. Apparently this was a case of blatant cultural appropriation, a sin akin to murder. The words 'prostitution' and 'degrading' were freely bandied about before Shanille finally said, quite rightly, I thought, "*I'm* the conductor here, so *I'm* the one who decides, and I've decided that tonight we're singing *Cats*, cultural appropriation or not!"

"Aren't we always singing cats, Max?" asked Dooley.

"Yes, but tonight we're singing cats that are singing *Cats*," I said, earning myself a confused frown from my best friend. I didn't blame him. It was all very complicated.

For one thing, apparently in this musical it was actually humans pretending to be cats, by putting on costumes and wearing makeup and such. So now we were cats pretending to be humans pretending to be cats. I think no one could blame me for feeling an identity crisis coming on. It was the cultural appropriation of the cultural appropriation by the culturally appropriated, which probably canceled the whole thing out. Or something.

And then of course there was the murder case I was still struggling with. The identity of Valina Fawn's murderer wasn't anywhere near being revealed to us, even after all the interviews Odelia and Chase had carried out. On the contrary. The more people we talked to, the muddier the whole thing seemed to become.

Then again, in this stage of the proceedings, that was often the case.

And we'd just taken our positions, when suddenly a loud voice started tweeting in our rear.

"Harriet, oh, sweet Harriet," the voice sounded. "You are mine and I am yours forever!"

We all turned to see, and found ourselves staring at none other than Jack the sparrow, perched on an overhanging branch, and singing his heart out and serenading Harriet!

"Oh, not you again!" Harriet cried, looking extremely embarrassed.

"But I love you!" said the tiny brown sparrow. "Our love is written in the stars!"

Dooley glanced up at this, inspecting the stars for a sign of this unusual love.

"I didn't know you had a new boyfriend, Harriet?" said Shanille, who seemed to think the whole thing hilarious.

"He is not my boyfriend," Harriet said through gritted teeth.

"I am your bird-friend!" Jack cried. "Your one true love!"

"Oh, go away," said Harriet. "Go tweet somewhere else."

"I won't be apart from you, Harriet," Jack replied, pressing a tiny foot to his tiny chest. "From now on we'll never be apart again. Our love will stand the test of time—forever."

"Oh, God," Harriet muttered, closing her eyes.

"I didn't know you were into birds?" said Shanille, grinning wickedly.

"I'm not," Harriet snapped. "And now could we please take it from the top!"

"He looks yummy," said Kingman, who's one of our larger members. He was licking his lips at the sight of Jack tweeting up a storm now, doing his utmost to let his love be known to all the world. "Not much flesh to his bones, maybe, but a nice dessert nonetheless."

"Please don't eat him, Kingman," I said. "Can't you see the bird is in love?"

"So? It might add to his aroma."

Harriet, absolutely mortified now, as the entire cat congregation of Hampton Cove was all atwitter and loudly chuckling and cracking off-color jokes at her expense, now hissed, "Jack! Go away! Before one of these cats gets it into their nut to come up there and eat you!"

"See!" Jack twittered. "You do love me. Otherwise you wouldn't try to save me!"

"Nobody try to eat Harriet's new boyfriend!" Shanille called out, a smirk on her face.

"How many times?! He's not my boyfriend!" Harriet snapped.

Some cats were making kissy noises now, and it was obvious the thing was quickly getting out of paw. Jack, oblivious to the turmoil he was causing in the heart of cat choir, simply kept on tweeting loudly, and declaring his undying love for our Persian friend.

Finally Kingman couldn't control himself any longer, and started to climb the tree Jack was perched in. He got as far as the first branch, then got stuck. "Heeeeelp! Someone save me!" he bleated.

"Just jump, Kingman," I said. "You're not that high up."

"I'm afraid to, Max! Please do something!"

To add insult to injury, Jack had now tiptoed down the branch until he was almost within reach of Kingman, who was holding onto the branch for dear life, and eyed the cat with beady eyes. "Are you a friend of Harriet, sir?" the tiny sparrow asked, cocking his head just so.

Kingman nodded staunchly. "I am. One of her best friends."

"That's all right, then. Any friend of my one true love is a friend of mine," said Jack.

Kingman glanced down, then swallowed with difficulty. "Good to know."

"And if you want, I can show you how to get down from this tree."

"Oh, would you? That's so very kind of you, Mr. Bird."

"The name is Jack," said Jack. "Jack the sparrow."

"Odd," said Kingman, frowning. "That name rings a bell for some reason. So how do I get down from here, Jack?"

"You simply spread your wings and fly!" Jack cried, and to show us how it was done, he did just that. He spread his wings, fluttered up to Kingman, who started violently, uttered a sort of high cry of shock... and dropped down from the tree.

Luckily he landed on all fours, and after checking himself for any sign of injuries, gave Jack a very frosty look. "Thanks for nothing, buddy!" he yelled, shaking an irate fist.

"You're welcome, friend of Harriet," said Jack, fully oblivious of the cat's ire. "And remember: love is always the way!"

And then, much to Harriet's elation, he flew off.

"I don't like your new boyfriend, Harriet," Kingman grumbled, starting to lick himself.

"He is not my boyfriend!" Harriet screamed.

Next to me, Brutus had silently materialized. He now

gave me a nudge. “Check that tablet, Max. Somehow I have a feeling the lady doth protest too much!”

And so it was that I suddenly realized I’d landed myself in the middle of a scene that could have featured in *Cats*! So maybe this Andrew Lloyd Webber fellow had indeed taken the measure of a cat: drama, more drama… and yet even more drama.

CHAPTER 17

The next morning, the investigation continued, and we found ourselves back in the offices of Valina Fawn. Valina's office was still off limits, with yellow crime scene tape attached to the door, and the person we were there to see this time was Meghan Fray, Valina's personal assistant.

After going through both membership lists of the Brookwell Archery Club and the dating site, an eagle-eyed member of Chase's team had discovered another overlap between the two lists: Valina Fawn herself.

"Oh, absolutely," said Meghan when questioned about her deceased boss's fondness for the sport of archery. "She went there all the time. Though if you ask me, she wasn't into the sport itself but more into one of the club members." She arched a meaningful and finely penciled eyebrow at this.

"You mean Valina was having an affair with one of Brookwell's members?" asked Odelia, immediately interested.

"Oh, yes, and a pretty torrid one from the looks of things.

I caught them at it, you see. Right here in her office. I was working late one night and I'd gone to the bathroom. When I came back I heard sounds of a couple... well, going at it, to put it bluntly. I think he must have come in and figured I'd already left and they were alone in the building."

"So you discreetly left and made sure you gave your boss the privacy you felt she deserved," said Chase dryly.

Meghan shot him an 'are you kidding me' look and said, "I went into the adjacent office and quietly opened the door to take a peek. I mean what else do you expect me to do? Valina had just told me that after running a dating site for years she didn't believe in love anymore, and how she'd decided she was going to remain single for the rest of her life. And now here she was, moaning down the whole building!"

"And so what did you see?" asked Odelia eagerly.

"Norwell Kulhanek."

"You gotta be kidding!"

"No, I swear to God! They were on her desk doing—"

"Yes, yes, we don't need to hear all the sordid details," said Chase. "So Valina and Norwell were an item? Are you sure?"

"Absolutely. Though for what it's worth, it didn't last long. This was about a month ago, and a week later they fell out. Huge fight."

"What about?"

"I'm not sure, but I'm guessing she probably dumped him and he didn't take it well." She gave Odelia a knowing look. "We all know that men have a very fragile ego, and Norwell's ego is as fragile as a bird's egg. So if she dumped him, he probably blew up."

"I see," said Chase, nodding.

"But what did he expect? The guy is married, after all. With two kids, no less. He probably wanted more than just a casual fling and she told him she wasn't interested. Valina may have been a lot of things, but she wasn't a homewrecker, whatever people say."

"Is he in, Norwell?" asked Chase.

"Nah, he's in New York today. Meeting with investors. He's trying to salvage what's left of the site now that Valina's gone." She sighed. "Fat lot of good that'll do. This place is a goner, from what I can tell. Valina was the heart and soul of this place. With her dead it's just an empty shell. If I'm smart I'll pack my bags and quit while I still can. Pretty soon the last of the money will run out and I can say goodbye to any severance pay."

"Thank you for telling us, Meghan," said Odelia. "But why didn't you mention this yesterday?"

Meghan shrugged. "I didn't think it was important. But then I spent all last night thinking things through, and finally I figured that maybe he's the one that did her in, you know. If he took her breaking things off badly, he might have decided that if he couldn't have her, no one would."

"It's a thought," Odelia admitted, "though the man has a solid alibi. His wife claims he was home all night."

"Mh," said Meghan, giving Odelia a skeptical look.

"You think she might be lying?"

"Wouldn't be the first wife caught in a lie, would she? I know women like Emma Kulhanek. They know full well that their husband is a liar and a cheat but still they stand by him whatever happens. Some twisted idea of loyalty. Hoping he'll reward them for their lies by staying with them. Which of course they never do. Oh, by the way, I found this on my desk this morning." She produced a key card and handed it to Chase.

"This is Norwell's key card," the cop said with a frown.

"Yeah, you told me yesterday it had gone missing, remember?"

"Where did you find it, exactly?"

"On my desk. Someone must have found it and dropped it there."

"Any idea who?"

She shook her head. "No idea. One of the cleaners, maybe?"

Chase nodded. "Thanks, Meghan."

"You're welcome." She gave him a fervent look. "I really hope you catch the bastard that did this. Valina wasn't everyone's cup of tea, but I liked her. She was tough to work for, but fair. She always treated me like a human being, you know, not like some slave." She frowned, dragging a groove across her smooth brow. "That's probably what killed her."

"What is?"

"Valina was nobody's fool. She was a self-made woman who turned this site into a great success. And if there's one thing a lot of men don't like, it's a successful woman."

"You think the hack and the murder are connected?" asked Odelia.

"Wouldn't surprise me one bit. First they destroy her business, then they destroy her." She nodded. "If I were you, I'd take a close look at Norwell, whatever his wife says."

And talking about the devil, just then Norwell came breezing into the office, looking pale and tired.

Which was exactly the time to pounce on the man. Or so Chase must have thought, for he didn't even allow the guy to shrug out of his coat.

"A word, please, Mr. Kulhanek?" the cop said immediately.

The man looked annoyed. "Can't we do this later? I just returned from a grueling commute and an even more grueling meeting."

But Chase fixed him with a piercing look. "Now, Mr. Kulhanek."

Norwell swallowed, then nodded. "Let's go into my office," he said, darting a quick glance to Meghan, who regarded the man coldly.

CHAPTER 18

"We found this," said Chase, placing the key card on the man's desk. The cop had put the card in a small plastic bag, and Norwell now picked it up.

"My key card," he said, fingering the trifle. "Where did you find it?"

"It was on Meghan Fray's desk this morning when she arrived for work. Did you put it there?"

"Me? I told you I lost it."

"So you say," said Chase. "Is it true, Mr. Kulhanek, that you and Valina Fawn were having an affair until three weeks ago?"

"An affair!" the man cried, clearly taken aback. "Who gave you that idea?"

But Chase and Odelia were both staring at the man intently.

"Of course I wasn't having an affair. I'm a happily married man, detective."

"And yet we have a witness who saw you and Valina engaged in what can only be described as a lovers clinch one late night at the office about a month ago."

Norwell gulped, as his eyes nervously shifted between Chase and Odelia. "I don't know what to say," he finally said.

"Please don't lie to us, Mr. Kulhanek," said Chase quietly but with a hint of menace.

"I'm not…" He gulped again, then glanced to a portrait of himself with his wife and their two kids. They were two girls, kindergartners still. "Look… can I… count on your discretion?"

"That depends."

"On what?"

"On whether your affair has any bearing on our investigation."

"I can't see how it does."

"So you admit you and Valina were having an affair."

He lowered his gaze and slowly nodded.

"How long did this affair last?"

"Not long. A couple of weeks—a month, maybe. I wouldn't even call it an affair. We… just got together a few times. Always at the office, and always after hours. I guess… the stress of trying to build the site… it drew us close together. And we both needed some kind of release, I guess you could call it. It was just a physical thing—nothing more."

"And yet when Valina broke it off you blew up, didn't you? Became very upset."

"Who told you…"

"The truth this time, Norwell!"

"Yes, yes—I did get upset when she told me she wanted to end it. I thought she'd developed feelings for me, you see, and when she said it was purely physical from her side, I just… lost it, I guess."

"And so you decided to kill her, didn't you? For making a fool out of you!"

The man looked up, his lips quivering. "No! No, of course not!"

"You're lying again, Norwell."

"No, I'm telling you the truth! I didn't kill her. Okay, so I was upset. Who wouldn't be? I thought she liked me. But she just used me. Like a plaything. Some toy she fooled around with for a while, until she got tired and brushed me aside. I felt hurt and... humiliated and angry, yes. But I would never harm her. I... well, I loved her," he concluded quietly.

"What about your wife?"

"I love my wife," he said staunchly. "But in a different way. More like... a friend."

"A friend."

"Yes! I don't know how long you've been married, detective, but after a while that passion, it just fizzles out, and is replaced by a deep, abiding feeling of kinship. But sometimes a man needs to feel that heat—that animal lust. And that's what I felt with Valina. Oh, God, the woman drove me mad. But I was never going to leave Emma. I mean, we have two kids, for God's sake. We've built something together—a family. A home."

"A home you couldn't wait to leave so you could play out your fantasy with your boss," said Chase tersely.

"Valina wasn't my boss. We were partners," said Norwell. "Equals."

"I think you better tell us exactly what happened two nights ago," said Odelia gently. "And this time no lies please, Norwell."

The IT man nodded. "I was upset, because of the hack, but also about the fact that since Valina had broken up with me there was this distance between us. This cold civility. I desperately wanted to see her. Let her know how I felt. So I went down to the office."

"What time was this?" asked Chase.

"Midnight. Em had just gone to bed. I'd told her I'd sleep in the spare bedroom so I wouldn't wake her up. She had to get up early, you see. She was working in the morning, same as me, but also had to get the kids ready for school. Just after midnight I just couldn't take it anymore. I had to see Valina. So I headed down to the office, knowing she'd probably still be there. Only when I arrived, I discovered I'd left my key card at home—or at least I thought I had. So I phoned her."

"Valina."

"But she didn't pick up. I could see that the light in her office was on, so I figured she was still mad with me about the hack. I stuck around for a while." He hesitated, looking shamefaced now. "Like some stupid schoolboy I even threw pebbles at her window, hoping she'd let me in. But there was no response, so then I decided I was acting like an idiot, got into my car and left. I ended up driving around for a while, then went home."

"So Emma lied when she said you were home all night."

"She wouldn't have known I left. I was careful not to make a sound."

"Wouldn't she have heard you taking the car out of the garage?"

"I parked the car on the street."

"So you knew you were going out again. You'd planned this out before."

He nodded, not meeting their eyes. "I already told you. I felt this overpowering urge to talk to Valina without anyone else present. I thought if I could just see her—just the two of us—maybe things between us could be like before, you know."

Chase eyed the man with no sign of compassion. "I think you're still lying, Norwell. I think you entered the building that night, and tried to patch things up with Valina. Maybe you got rough when she told you that it was over. And this time you killed her, placing that Cupid doll on her body to make it look as if a disgruntled client or investor had done it."

"No!" said Norwell. "I swear I would never hurt her. I loved her too much. Adored her. And now she's gone... and I'll never be able to hold her in my arms again." And at this point, the man broke down and started weeping like a child.

For a moment Chase was torn between placing handcuffs on the man, or handing him a tissue. Finally he opted for a tissue, and when we left the office, Norwell was still sobbing, the broken wreck of a man.

CHAPTER 19

"I don't think I've ever seen a man cry like that, Max," said Dooley. "I didn't even know that men could cry."

"Of course men can cry," I said.

"I thought they didn't have tear ducts. If you don't have tear ducts, you can't cry."

"Now why wouldn't men have tear ducts?"

Dooley shrugged. "I just figure men are different, you know. Less sensitive."

"Men might like to think that they're impervious to the finer feelings, but they're not," I said. "Just look at Brutus. He was crying last night, wasn't he?"

"Yes, but Brutus is not a man, he's a cat."

Now there was a sample of sound reasoning I couldn't argue with. When we'd arrived home last night, well ahead of Harriet and Brutus, I'd checked Harriet's tablet, and discovered that contrary to what she'd claimed, she hadn't canceled her Pettr account. On the contrary, I could tell that she'd been very active, chatting with several pets that might be described as 'boyfriend material' by connoisseurs. When I subsequently told Brutus, his eyes had gone all moist, and more than one tear had flowed from his eyes.

"But why, Max!" he'd cried. "Why did she deceive me!"

"I'm not sure," I said. "Though her chats are all pretty innocuous if you ask me. Just your usual 'Hi, how are you' kind of stuff. Nothing too passionate or suspicious."

"Still," he said quietly, and had then sort of slumped off, the picture of a broken cat.

"Poor Brutus," said Dooley now. "It must be tough for him to know that Harriet is cheating on him with some other cat."

"We don't know that, Dooley," I said. "All we know for sure is that she's on Pettr and has been chatting up a storm with several potential suitors."

"Maybe she's like Norwell: she feels Brutus is more like a friend than a boyfriend after all the time they've been together. Like a warm blanket at night, you know, or a hot-water bottle, but not exactly the kind of lover that sets your heart and soul alight."

I frowned at my friend. "Please don't mention your 'hot-water bottle' theory to Brutus. Unless you want to make him cry again."

"Oh, of course not. Though it's obvious we have to do something, Max. After all, if Harriet decides to get involved with another cat, things are going to get very awkward for all of us."

The thought had occurred to me. It's hard to go from being a couple to being mere friends, especially when you're living together under the same roof. And even harder when a fifth member would suddenly insert themselves into our lives.

The car was speeding along, though Chase made sure, as he always did, to respect the speed limit. Which is odd, since as a cop he is allowed to switch on that flashy thing and proceed through traffic at a high rate of speed. But I guess we weren't in a high-speed pursuit right now, chasing some suspect, so a more pedestrian pace was satisfactory.

"We should talk to Harriet," said Dooley now. "And find out what's going on."

"I know, but first we need to make sure we catch her alone. It might be awkward if Brutus is there. And besides, she'll probably go for staunch denial if we confront her."

"So we have to break her down, Max. We'll have to take a page from Chase's book. Like he broke down Norwell, and made him tell the truth, we have to make Harriet confess all."

"And how do you propose we do that? Harriet is no Norwell Kulhanek, Dooley. She's made of much sterner stuff. In fact the only way you break down Harriet's defense is if you're a man of iron." Or a cat of iron, for that matter.

"So we adopt the good cop, bad cop routine. You'll be the good cop, and I'll be the bad one."

I studied my friend. His natural cheerfulness, his guileless countenance. "What makes you think you can be the bad cop?" I asked finally.

"It's all about throwing Harriet off balance, Max," he said, his excitement palpable. "If you're going to start shouting at her, she'll simply brush you off, since she's used to that kind of behavior. But what if I start shouting at her? She'll be so shocked she'll immediately break down and tell us everything."

"Mh," I said, not fully convinced, though I could see where he was coming from. The surprise attack.

"Just you wait and see. I'll make her talk."

I smiled. "Tough guy, huh?" I said.

"You better believe it!" And he gave me a sort of Clint Eastwood squint. Though coming from him it looked more as if he had something in his eyes. Like a fruit fly.

We'd arrived at what looked like a school, and when I

looked closer I saw that indeed it was such an institution, for I saw several hundred kids milling about behind a fence. There was of course a chance that it was a POW camp, but even though they looked pretty bored and bad-tempered, they also looked too well fed and well-dressed to be inmates.

"What are we doing here?" I asked Odelia, for I may be a broad-minded cat, able to get along with any creature, from rat to raven, but I firmly draw the line at teenagers, which are possibly the most noxious species ever created by an otherwise benevolent God.

"We're going to have another chat with Emma Kulhanek," Odelia explained.

Of course. Emma was a teacher, wasn't she? And what better place to interview a teacher than in their natural habitat?

We passed through long, deserted corridors, filled with lockers and that strange odor that your garden-variety teenager spreads: a certain mustiness mixed with cheap deodorant, until we found the teacher's room. We patiently waited outside, while Chase ventured into the lion's den, and soon returned with Emma, who looked appropriately concerned. When the constabulary pays you a visit at work, it must be serious.

"What's wrong?" she asked immediately, and I could tell she knew Odelia hadn't come here to discuss the next book club meeting.

She led us into an empty classroom, which was filled with all manner of strange contraption: test tubes and glass jars filled with mysterious liquids, and we all took a seat around a student desk. Or at least the humans took their seats, while Dooley and I decided to inspect the classroom, going for a clockwise inspection along the perimeter, as cats do.

And while we sniffed all the peculiar odors that permeated the space, Chase launched his first salvo. "You lied to us,

Emma. Norwell wasn't home all night like you said. He left the house at midnight and didn't return until much later."

Emma's mouth opened and then closed again, fear etched on her features and reflected in her eyes. "I-I-I," she stuttered —never a good sign.

"Did you know he left the house?" asked Odelia, adopting a kinder tone.

Tears had suddenly sprung into Emma's eyes and she now pressed them closed and nodded furiously.

"So why didn't you tell us?"

"I thought if I did, it might cause trouble for Norwell."

"By not telling us you caused a lot more trouble for your husband," said Chase sternly.

"I know. I'm sorry."

"So tell us what actually happened that night," said Odelia.

Dooley and I had returned from our inspection and now sat at the woman's feet, studying her intently. They say you can tell if a person lies from the tone of their voice and their facial expression, but I've found that this isn't necessarily true. There are some skilled liars out there, who can look and sound truthful while still concocting one lie after another. Still, I like to think I'm as fine a feline lie detector as has ever walked the earth, and I was determined to put my skill to the test now.

"Norwell had told me he was going to work late, and not to wait up. So I'd gone to bed and fallen asleep. I woke up in the middle of the night, and when I looked at my alarm clock I saw that it was close to two o'clock. I heard a key in the lock, and then I heard how Norwell walked up the stairs and went into the bathroom, then into the spare bedroom. So I knew he'd left the house at some point." She directed a pleading look at Odelia. "But I swear I didn't know where he'd gone."

"You didn't ask him about it in the morning?"

She shook her head. "I just figured he'd gone for a walk. He's been under a lot of pressure lately, with this hack, and he's been working much too hard. I didn't want to add more pressure by questioning him."

"But when you heard about what happened to Valina you must have wondered, surely," said Chase.

"I did, but there's simply no way that Norwell would do a horrible thing like that. He's a sweet man. He can't even kill a spider. He always captures it in a jar and puts it out."

"There are serial killers out there that wouldn't hurt a fly," said Chase, "but don't bat an eye when they're filleting a human being or burying a person alive."

"Norwell isn't a serial killer, detective. He's a good, kind man. A wonderful husband and a great father. So to think that he could murder... It's simply beyond the realm of possibility."

Chase and Odelia shared a glance, then decided to lay all of their cards on the table. It was simply too important to ignore. "This may come as a shock to you, Emma," said Chase, "but we've just discovered this morning that Norwell and Valina were having an affair."

Emma's eyes went wide as saucers, and her face drained of blood, turning a sickly white. "W-w-what?" she stammered as she brought a distraught hand to her mouth.

"The affair ended three weeks ago," said Odelia. "By all accounts it was a brief fling."

"At least to Valina it was a fling," said Chase, intent on twisting the knife. "To Norwell it was more than a fling, and he was clearly heartbroken when Valina ended it."

"But—surely that's not possible," said Emma. "You're not serious?"

"I'm afraid we are," said Odelia kindly. She'd placed a hand on the other woman's arm.

Emma's eyes now turned to the window, but it was clear

she wasn't seeing the clear blue sky or even the sun as it rose ever tirelessly higher. Her skin had become almost translucent now, and I had the impression she was on the verge of a nervous collapse.

"I don't understand," she said finally, a wobble in her voice. "Norwell and... Valina?"

Odelia nodded. "I'm sorry we had to spring this on you, Emma, but it's important that you tell us if you knew about the affair? Ever noticed anything? Strange phone calls, maybe, or Norwell hiding things from you?"

But Emma was shaking her head, and it was obvious that this had come as a complete surprise to her. "I thought he didn't like her," she said finally. "I thought they were like cats and dogs. Always arguing, at loggerheads. I even told him he should be more kind to her. Suggested we all have dinner together one night. That it was important they get along. And all this time..." Her voice died away.

"Could be that he simply pretended to dislike her," said Chase. "Classic trick of a person trying to hide an affair. Make you think they don't like the other person."

"She was tough on him," said Emma, trying to collect herself with a powerful effort. "Extremely critical of his work. But then again, that's simply how she was, Valina. She was a very demanding person, not just for others but also for herself. Nothing was ever good enough. She really pushed herself, and others, to the limit. I felt bad for the people who worked for her, Norwell included." She looked up. "I spearhead the anti-bullying campaign here at school, you see. It's very important for us to make these kids aware that bullying simply won't do, and we strive hard to make this a school that says no to bullies. It's a project that's very close to my heart, and so when I heard Norwell complain about Valina, I never imagined they would..." Tears sprang to her eyes afresh. "That they were..."

"It's all right," said Odelia, rubbing the woman's back.

"Oh, God," sobbed Emma, and I saw we were in hugging territory now. Not one of my strong suits, I must admit. Still, I could tell that the woman wasn't deceitful in the slightest, and so I decided to do my bit and gave her a nudge against the leg and so did Dooley.

"Poor woman," said Dooley once Chase had been dispatched to forage around for a box of tissues. "It's just one shock after another, isn't it?"

"Yeah, must be terrible to find out about your husband's unfaithfulness this way."

Then again, any way to find out something like that is bad, of course.

"Do you think they'll get a divorce now, Max?"

"I don't know, Dooley. They might patch things up again, you know. Human relationships are resilient. It all depends how deep Norwell's feelings for Valina were."

A couple of kids had drifted into the classroom, and when they saw their teacher's tears, just stood there gawking for a moment, like cows at a train, but then Chase returned, and wasted no time turning the kids away again and closing the door.

The last thing Emma needed was for her students to find out about this cheating business.

After we left, impressing upon the woman to get in touch when she could think of anything that might shed more light on her husband's behavior toward Valina, we drifted through those same corridors again, only this time they were being overrun with more teenagers than I'd ever seen in my life. I must say I'm not a scaredy cat by any means, but when I saw that mass of seething teens, I momentarily feared for my life. When they saw us, they jeered, they pointed, they called us some very unkind names, and generally they seemed to think us the funniest double act since Laurel and Hardy, for they couldn't stop laughing all the way until we finally reached safety and burst out into the open again.

"Those were probably the scariest ten minutes of my entire life," I confessed to Dooley.

"Me, too!" Dooley cried.

"Teenagers are the worst."

"Worse than vampires or zombies?"

"There's no such thing as vampires or zombies, Dooley."

"If there were, I think I'd prefer their company to teenagers every day, Max."

The most important thing was that we'd entered the pit of doom and made it out in one piece. Poor Emma, though. She was still in there. Worse, she was in there every day!

What a brave soul. To risk life and limb on a daily basis to try and turn a bunch of hormonal hooligans into more or less decent human beings. Talk about a mission impossible!

CHAPTER 20

We'd only just returned to the safety of the car, when a call came in about a domestic disturbance.

"Ten-seven," Gran's voice crackled over the radio. "Come in, over."

"Yes, this is Chase, Vesta," said Chase with a grin to Odelia. "What seems to be the trouble?"

"There's a couple trying to kill each other on Beneficent Avenue. I think you'd better take a look before one of them draws blood."

"Got a name for me?" asked Chase as he turned the key in the ignition.

There was silence on the other end, then: "Are you trying to be funny, sonny? This is Vesta. And if you don't know my name by now, I think it's high time that you learned it."

"Not your name, Gran," said Odelia, speaking into the receiver. "The name of the people involved in the domestic dispute."

"Oh, right. Um…" There was a rustle of paper as she consulted her notes. "That's a Lynnette and Franco Say. And according to the neighbor who called it in, Lynnette was heard threatening her husband. The words 'cheat,' 'ax, 'chop' and 'nuts' were mentioned."

"Got it," said Chase. "We're heading out there now."

"Ten-thirteen," said Gran, and disconnected.

"What's ten-thirteen?" asked Odelia. "Or ten-seven?"

"Ten-thirteen is the weather-road report and ten-seven is out of service." He grinned. "Looks like she's got her numbers mixed up."

This time Chase did turn on that flashy light, and even the siren, and as we zoomed through traffic, zigzagging where zigzagging was required, and going at breakneck speed where possible, we made good time.

"Isn't Lynnette Say a member of Marge's book club?" asked Dooley as we held on for dear life, embedding our nails deeply into the backseat as one is wont to do under these hair-raising circumstances.

"Yeah, she is. She's the one who said that if a man cheats on a woman it's her own darn fault, because she didn't give him what he needed, or something along those lines."

"Interesting," said Dooley. "I wonder what Lynnette didn't give Franco that he would have cheated on her. Enough potatoes during dinner, maybe, or a lack of attention?"

"In my experience, Dooley, a woman can give a man everything he needs and more and he still might cheat on her."

"So are all men cheaters, Max, do you think?"

"I don't know, Dooley, but I'm starting to lean toward that point of view."

What was obvious was that the hack of Valina's site had revealed a seedy underbelly to our local community that was far more shocking than anyone might have assumed.

It didn't take us long to arrive at the street where the Says lived, and even as we got out of the car, we could already see a small group of neighbors having gathered on the front lawn, and could hear Mr. and Mrs. Say exchanging some particularly harsh words.

"You're a dirty rotten bastard, Franco Say!" Lynnette was saying.

"Please let me explain, Lynnette!" Franco said.

"I don't want to hear it!"

We hurriedly rounded the house, and found the feuding couple in the backyard, with a stocky neighbor merely dressed in cargo shorts and a sleeveless T-shirt watching on stoically. "I found them in bed together," the man now announced. "Him and my wife."

"How could you do this to me!" Lynnette howled, then made to attack her husband. Chase held her back, and I saw that the cowering Franco had already sustained some injuries: he had a black eye, and several bloodied scratches on his face. Clearly we'd gotten there just in time to prevent more serious damage to be sustained by either party.

Odelia led Lynnette away from her husband, and the woman broke down on a lounge chair next to the pool. "Rex found Franco in bed with Marcie," she explained, "and called me. Looks like it's been going on for some time."

"Marcie is..."

"Rex's wife."

"Is he the one who gave Franco that black eye?"

Lynnette nodded. "He should have given him two black eyes. And you know the worst part? He's not even sorry! Said it's only natural for a man to have urges. Urges!"

"There, there," said Odelia, patting the woman's arm. She'd squatted next to the lounge chair and now glanced over to where Chase was talking to her husband. Franco was pressing a piece of cloth to his bruised and scratched face, the neighbor still looking on with that same stoic expression on his face, as if this was a regular thing for him.

"What do you want to do, Lynnette?" asked Odelia. "Do you want to stay here or..."

"Of course I'm going to stay here! You are going to arrest him, aren't you? Lock him up?" She darted a hopeful look in Chase's direction.

"Adultery is not a punishable offense," Odelia pointed out.

"Well, it should be! That man deserves to be hung, drawn and quartered!"

It took a while for the mess to be sorted out, but finally Franco agreed to go and stay with his brother, while Lynnette would stay on at the house. The couple's kids were at school, so it was important that one of their parents was there when they arrived home.

Lynnette now burst into tears and Franco cried, "I'm sorry, Lynn! It was an accident!"

"Of course it was," said the neighbor, still leaning over the fence. "He accidentally fell into my bed and on top of my wife."

We watched Franco drive off, and then took leave ourselves. And we had just stepped into the car, when the radio crackled to life once more.

"Ten-forty-five," Gran's irascible voice sounded. "Come in, over."

"What is it, Vesta?" asked Chase, grabbing the receiver.

"Got another one for you."

"Another what?"

"Another ten-fifty-four!"

Chase grinned. "Animal carcass on the road? Or livestock on the highway?"

"What are you talking about? Another couple threatening to kill each other. Carlotta and Dennis Brook over at the Brookwell Artery Club."

"You mean the archery club?"

"Whatever. I don't know if it's something in the water or what, but people are going nuts all over the place today."

"We'll go and take a look," Chase acknowledged.

"Better get a move on. According to the guy who called it in she was threatening to shoot him—with bow and arrow, if you please. Just like the Valina Fawn woman!"

CHAPTER 21

As Vesta disconnected, she glanced over to Scarlett, who was watching a TikTok video of a dancing penguin. "I don't know what this world is coming to," she grumbled. "Second domestic dispute of the day, and both of them members of my daughter's book club."

"Bad for your health, books," said Scarlett, without looking up.

"So how did I do?"

"What do you mean?"

"Did I show enough empathy, you reckon?"

"Oh, sure," said Scarlett. "Though maybe you shouldn't have told that first guy that the police can't be bothered with men cheating on their wives."

"I didn't know she was trying to kill him, did I?"

"Honey, I think it's a safe bet that when they call 911 it's important. So next time you simply give them the benefit of the doubt, all right?"

"Fine," she grouched. "This whole empathy business is a tough nut to crack."

"Hard to change a habit of a lifetime," Scarlett agreed. "But if anyone can do it, it's you."

"Grrr," said Vesta. She wasn't fully convinced. In her view the world consisted of two kinds of people: the ones she liked and the ones she couldn't be bothered with. Unfortunately, and through no fault of her own, there were only a handful of the former, and a whole lot of the latter. It wasn't a judgment on her part, but simply the way the world worked. Some people would have called her a grinch, or even a misanthrope, but in actual fact she was simply a realist. Then again, it probably wasn't a bad idea to consider the notion that there were more good people out there than she had always thought.

A bold idea, but one she was willing to take into consideration. Especially now that she was the official Hampton Cove PD dispatcher. A job with responsibility and even, one might say, a certain authority. Almost like being a cop.

She perked up at this. Wasn't being a cop like being the boss of all people? And being the boss, wasn't she entitled to the respect and the appreciation that came with the territory?

If that was true, she could probably afford to be a little nicer to people. After all, lions are known to be nice to any antelope crossing their path. Especially when they've just started ripping it to shreds and snacking on its innards.

"I'm king of the world," she now murmured, earning herself a strange look from Scarlett, which she pointedly ignored. She could be nice. She grinned before herself, practicing her smile. It made her cheeks hurt for some reason. Probably because she was using muscles she hadn't practiced in years. Also, her dentures suddenly felt clickety.

"Why are you looking like a serial killer all of a sudden?" asked Scarlett.

"I'm trying to be nice," said Vesta, grimacing even wider.

"Well, don't," said Scarlett. "You're scaring me."

"Everyone's a critic," she grumbled.

When we arrived at the Brookwell Archery Club, Mrs. Brook was standing perfectly poised with bow and arrow, the picture of the Olympic champion. Only she wasn't aiming at a target but at her husband, who stood, arms akimbo and sweating profusely, staring at his wife and either hoping she'd never discovered his infidelity, or wishing he'd never been unfaithful in the first place.

"Carlotta, please put down that bow," Chase called out.

Several club members stood watching the scene, some of them with their phones out, filming everything. Probably so they could later turn it into a funny TikTok movie.

"He needs to confess first!" Carlotta said. "And apologize for his appalling behavior!"

"Look, I admit I may have strayed from the straight and narrow!" Dennis called out. "But only the one time!"

"You're lying. I can see it in your eyes, Dennis."

"I'm not lying! Honestly!"

"How many times?"

"Okay, so maybe it happened twice. But only twice!"

"Liar!"

"Three times!"

"He sounds like an auctioneer, Max," said Dooley, very aptly I thought.

"Liar!"

"Five times!" he cried, his final offer.

"Where!" Carlotta demanded.

"In the clubhouse," said Dennis.

"Do you love her?"

"No, of course not! I only love you, honey, you know that!"

"You bastard!" suddenly a voice sounded from the crowd of onlookers. It was a shortish woman dressed in a nice summer dress, showing a lot of tanned leg. "You told me you loved me! That you were going to divorce her and marry me!"

"Tanya?" said Carlotta, momentarily lowering her bow. "It was you?"

"I'm sorry, Carlotta," said Tanya. "He told me you were over."

The former Olympian's expression hardened, and she now aimed at the woman who'd just spoken. "I thought you were my friend!" she cried.

"I am your friend!" Tanya cried. "Please don't shoot me!"

"Put down your weapon!" Chase boomed, and this time his voice brooked no contest.

Carlotta wavered for a moment, then finally relented and relaxed the bow's string, lowering the arrow.

Both her husband and Tanya breathed a sigh of relief.

"I swear to God it's over, Carlotta," said Dennis.

"You piece of shit!" Tanya cried, and before anyone could stop her, had run over to Dennis and was pummeling the man with her fists, then kicking him where it hurt.

While Chase got busy releasing Dennis from his lover's fury, Odelia confiscated Carlotta's bow so she couldn't do any harm. And as she led Carlotta away, Chase talked to Dennis for a moment.

"Look, you have to understand," said the guy, as he watched Tanya stalk off on a huff in the direction of the clubhouse. "For a man in my position it's important to maintain friendly relations with the club's members. And sometimes you take things too far." He shrugged as he dusted himself off. "Is it my fault that I'm such a friendly guy?"

"Sounds to me like you were a little too friendly," said Chase, giving the man a disapproving look. Then he glanced over to Carlotta. "When did she find out?"

"This morning. Tanya and I have been texting, and Carlotta must have seen a message come in on my phone. Stupid of me, of course. I should have kept a separate phone." Chase's implacable and penetrating gaze must have hit its mark, for he amended, "I'm sorry. I'm a big jerk, I know. And there's absolutely no excuse for my behavior."

"No, there isn't," said Chase, still staring the man down.

Dennis now cowered slightly, wilting under that basilisk stare. "Okay, so I messed up! Show me the man who doesn't give in to temptation sometimes!"

"Just get lost, Dennis," Chase growled, and the man quickly skedaddled. A call now came in on Chase's mobile, and he listened for a moment, then cursed under his breath. When Odelia finally joined him a few moments later, he said, "They've found a bow and arrow in Lynnette and Franco Say's garden shed. They've arrested them both."

"You asked your people to search the shed?"

Chase nodded. "Looks like we've got more suspects now than we know what to do with, babe." He stared hard at Dennis Brook, then seemed to make up his mind and raised his phone to his lips again. "Send a unit to the Brookwell Archery Club, will you? And take both Carlotta and Dennis Brook into custody on suspicion of the murder of Valina Fawn."

CHAPTER 22

The precinct lockup had rarely seen as much activity as it was seeing today: two couples had been arrested and placed in the station slammer, and now all four of those people had to be interviewed, a task that Chase was prepared to engage in with relish. But since the man couldn't very well clone himself, and time was obviously of the essence, Uncle Alec had agreed to share the burden.

"Time you went to police academy and made things official," the Chief told his niece as he got ready to enter one of the interview rooms.

Odelia smiled at the big man. "Or you could simply allow me to sit in on your interviews."

"No can do, I'm afraid. As much as it pains me to say, you're not a cop, honey." He took a deep breath. "Wish me luck."

"Maybe we should all go to police academy," said Dooley as we settled in to watch the interviews through the one-way mirror police stations the world over implement. "That way we could all wear our badges proudly and interview suspects whenever we want."

"I don't think they allow cats at police academy, Dooley," I said. "And besides, we could talk to suspects until we're blue in the face and it still wouldn't do us any good." Most humans, you see, stubbornly refuse to talk to cats for some reason. Only Odelia, Marge and Gran can understand us, though even they ignore us sometimes, when they don't like what we have to say.

Picture the scene if you will: on the left Chase was settling in to grill Franco Say, and on the right, Uncle Alec was shifting his bulk on his chair and making himself comfortable in front of Dennis Brook. Both men looked uneasy at the prospect of being interrogated, not as witnesses this time, but as full-blown suspects in a murder inquiry.

"So tell me, Franco," said Chase, opening proceedings, "what that bow and those arrows were doing in your garden shed."

The man shrugged. "Just some old junk we had lying around. I've been meaning to clean out the place for ages, only never got around to it, that's all."

"So who's the shooter in your family? You or Lynnette?"

The man turned shifty-eyed. "Is this a trick question? Do I need a lawyer?"

"Oh, for crying out loud, Franco. Just answer the damn question, will you?"

"Lynnette's," said the man quietly. "She used to be a member at Brookwell but gave up years ago. Said it wreaked havoc on her wrists and so she stopped."

"And how about you? Were you ever a member?"

"Nah, not me. Though I did join her for a couple of club activities. Brunches and barbecues. Never found the whole shooting thing appealing. Never saw the point."

Dooley laughed at this. "He didn't see the point, Max. The point of the arrow!"

"Very funny, Dooley," I said, then strained my ears to follow the conversation.

"So let's talk about your infidelity for a moment," said Chase. "You and Marcia, huh?"

Franco shrugged as he stared down at the table. "Not my finest hour, I must admit."

"How did you hook up? Through Valina Fawn?"

Franco looked up. "What do you mean? The woman is my neighbor, for God's sakes. I see her every day. And you gotta admit, detective, she's one hell of a woman."

"She's also your neighbor's wife."

"Yeah, I know, but she didn't seem to mind."

"Lynnette isn't so understanding, though, is she?"

"You know what Lynnette's problem is? She's too... perfect! That's right. With Lynnette everything has to be just so, and that goes for everything in her life, including me. And frankly I just couldn't take it anymore, detective. And with Marcia there's no pressure involved. She just likes me for... me. She doesn't want to change me, or make me look a certain way. With her it's just fun. Easy and fun. And my God, man, after twenty years of Lynnette fun and easy was like a breath of fresh air. Like being released from prison."

"Okay, so I was having an affair," said Dennis Brook. "Big deal. A man in my position, Chief, has certain responsibilities. People expect things from you when you run a club like Brookwell. They expect you to be sociable. A mixer, if you see what I mean. I was doing it for the club, for us—for Carlotta's future and the future of the kids."

"So you cheated on your wife for her sake and for your kids' sake?" asked Uncle Alec, studying the man with a look of incredulity.

"Absolutely! Marriage is all about give and take, Chief.

And engaging in close relations with certain female members of the club gave me the opportunity to give something of myself to the community Carlotta and I have built. And look what we got back in return: a thriving club, filled with happy members."

"I can't imagine the husbands of the women you had affairs with are going to be so happy."

"Oh, but they are. You see, I made their wives happy, which is bound to make them happy. Well, as long as they don't find out, of course," he allowed. He frowned. "They're not going to find out, are they, Chief? Cause that would probably ruin the ambiance."

"I'm afraid that ambiance was probably ruined when you and Carlotta argued about your cheating in front of the club's entire membership roster, wouldn't you say?"

Dennis thought about this for a moment. "That would be bad," he finally concluded.

Carlotta was still looking as seething with anger as she had before, only now her anger was directed at Uncle Alec instead of her husband. "I can't believe you had me locked up like some common criminal!" she cried, tapping the table with furious fingers. "What did I do?!"

"For one thing you threatened to kill your husband," said Uncle Alec, gazing back at the irate woman with absolute equanimity.

"Can you blame me?! The man was cheating on me with my best friend!"

"Multiple of your best friends, from what I understood," said the police chief.

Carlotta's jaw dropped. "What?"

"Your husband is a very generous man, Carlotta. And a very sociable man. He believes in spreading the joy, so he admitted to engaging in intimate relations with no less than a dozen female club members over the years."

Carlotta's mouth opened and closed a few times as her face turned slightly more red.

"He says he did it for the sake of the club," the Chief continued. "And for you and the kids, of course. He says he believes in creating the perfect ambiance."

"The perfect ambiance!"

Uncle Alec nodded, and I could tell from the twinkle in his eye he was enjoying himself. "It's one way of looking at things, of course. And you have to admit he made a lot of people very happy over the years, by sharing his joy with them, as he put it."

"Oh, that man is so dead!" she growled, balling her hands into fists.

"Please don't kill your husband, Carlotta," the Chief tut-tutted. "We do frown on homicide in this country, you know, even husbands who are serial adulterers."

"Can't I mess him up a little, Chief? Just a little?"

"I'm sorry, but no."

"I could shoot him through a non-vital body part."

"This is not a negotiation, Carlotta." Then he added," What body part did you have in mind?"

Carlotta quirked a meaningful eyebrow, and the Chief grinned.

"Out of the question," he said. "Absolutely not allowed, I'm afraid."

"Too perfect!" Lynnette practically screamed. "Oh, I'll show him perfect!"

"Please don't do anything rash, Lynnette," said Chase warningly.

"How long has this been going on?" she demanded.

"According to your husband it all started with some innocent flirtations across the backyard fence last summer, heated up during a joint mulching session in the fall, and collecting acorns in the winter, before blooming into a full-blown affair in the spring."

"How many times?" she asked, her breathing having become a little stertorous.

"Well..."

"How many!"

"Your husband said he hasn't exactly kept track, but at least three times a week over the course of several months, so..."

"I'm going to murder that man, and then I'm going to kick him, and then I'm going to murder him again, and then—"

"Yes, I get the picture," said Chase, holding up his hand. "And for the record, I feel at this point I should remind you that murder is a punishable offense."

"He's never going to see the kids again for as long as he lives, and of course I'll take the house, and his money, and his car, and, and, and I'll take his collection of bowling balls!"

"Franco has a collection of bowling balls?"

"Oh, yes, he has. Keeps them in his man cave in the basement. Polishes them every night." A malevolent light had appeared in her eyes. "You know what I'll do? I'll throw them out of the second-floor window. Smash them all up into little pieces! And then I'll take an ax to his pinball machine and chop that up into little pieces. And then—"

Chase cleared his throat. "That bow and those arrows we found. They're yours?"

Lynnette frowned. "Bow?"

"Yes, we found a bow and a quiver of arrows in the garden shed. According to Franco they belong to you, from when you were a member of the Brookwell Club."

"I didn't even know we still had those," she said.

"Look, even though obviously Franco didn't meet Marcia on Valina Fawn's site, I still have to ask you, Lynnette. Where were you two nights ago between midnight and two?"

"Where do you think I was? In bed with that no-good cheating husband of mine. And if you really think I'm saying this because I want to provide him with an alibi, think again. If there was any way I could throw him under the bus for Valina's murder, I'd do it in a heartbeat."

"I wasn't thinking about Franco, Lynnette. I was thinking about you."

Lynnette blinked, then laughed a forced sort of laugh. "Me! Why would I want to murder Valina!"

"Because you thought her site facilitated your husband's cheating?"

Lynnette pressed her perfect lips together until they formed a thin line. "Nonsense. The first inkling I had that Franco was cheating on me was when Rex told me he found them in bed together this afternoon. He said the moment he saw Franco's hairy ass sticking out from between Marcia's legs..." She looked away. "Let's just say I never for one moment saw this one coming, detective, and that is God's honest truth. And now if you'll excuse me," she said, getting up, "I have twenty bowling balls to destroy!"

CHAPTER 23

"Why was Franco's hairy ass sticking out from between his neighbor's legs, Max?" asked Dooley.

We were in Uncle Alec's office, with the Chief, his niece and Chase discussing recent events, and I could tell that Dooley had been thinking about this question ever since the interviews had ended.

"I've been trying to picture the scene," said my friend, "and I'm having trouble with the logistics. So his ass was there, and her legs were there, but where was the rest of them?"

"I really don't think you need to concern yourself with this, Dooley," I said, not feeling particularly in the mood to get into a detailed description of 'the deed,' to be honest.

"No, but if they were kissing, then why was his ass—"

"Let's talk about this some other time, shall we?" I suggested.

"Oh, all right," he said, but I could tell he wasn't satisfied with my prevarications.

"Okay, so what have we got?" said the Chief, "apart from two cheaters and two furious wives and what looks like a lot of cuckolded husbands, a dozen of whom are members of our local archery club, and one of whom runs our local gun store."

"I just hope there won't be thirteen murders about to be committed," said Chase with a frown. "Twelve with bow and arrow and one by shotgun."

"Yes, well, let's deal with that if and when it happens. For now we'll focus on Valina Fawn's murder. Who are our suspects and where are we with alibis and such?"

"Okay, so Chase's people have cross-referenced the membership list of Valina's site with that of the Brookwell Archery Club," said Odelia, "and came up with two dozen names."

Chief Alec grabbed his thinning mane and pulled hard. "This case is killing me!"

"Of those two dozen we've already interviewed a dozen, and so far we've managed to eliminate all of them," said Chase. "So only an even dozen left."

"Though of course," said Odelia, "our killer could be someone else entirely. Someone who is neither a member of the site or the archery club."

More hair-pulling was going on, and we all looked on with a touch of concern. The Chief doesn't have a lot of hair left to begin with, and this wasn't helping matters in that department. "When even the Mayor of this town is a suspect," said the big guy, "I think it's safe to say we're in trouble."

"Charlene is not a suspect, Chief," Chase assured him. "We talked to her and she's fine."

"Okay, so that still leaves too many balls in the air. We need to narrow it down, people," said Uncle Alec, pounding his desk with his fist. "And we need to do it fast. The longer this investigation drags on, the more difficult it becomes to nail our perp."

Two heads bowed as one, and both Chase and Odelia looked appropriately chastised.

"Okay, so if his ass was between her legs, where was his head, Max?" asked Dooley.

"Licking her toes, probably," I murmured as I gave this baffling case some thought.

"Did you say toes?" asked my friend.

"No, I didn't."

"I thought you said toes. Which is impossible, since if he was licking her toes, then she was… licking his toes and… is this really what humans get up to, Max? I mean, you hear strange stories, but this is just… plain weird."

"I know, Dooley," I said with a sigh. "I know."

"We've got people going through the Valina Fawn membership list with a fine-tooth comb," now Chase intoned. "Looking at anything out of the ordinary: criminal records, financial records, phone records…"

"You can't get away from the fact that whoever killed Valina gained access to the place by using Norwell Kulhanek's key card," said Uncle Alec. "And that the key card was returned to the desk of Valina's personal assistant the following day."

"Or even the night of the murder," said Odelia. "Since you only need a key card to access the building, not to leave it. So as I see it, the killer used Norwell's card to enter the building at one-fifteen, then left it on Meghan's desk after the murder."

Uncle Alec nodded. "Okay, so even though trawling through the site's membership list is a good idea, what we need here is focus. We need to narrow our search, not widen it. Who had access to Norwell on the day of the murder?

Since we know he had his key card on him that morning, whoever took it must have snatched it on the day."

"I'm still not convinced Norwell is in the clear," said Chase. "The man admits he left the house at midnight, drove to the office, claims he discovered his key card gone and couldn't get in, phoned Valina at twelve-thirty, who didn't pick up, then drove around aimlessly for a while, before returning home around two o'clock in the morning. Oh, and he was a member at Brookwell, so he knows how to handle bow and arrow."

"Even if he didn't do it, don't you find it odd that he didn't see the killer?" asked Odelia.

"He must have just missed him," Uncle Alec said. "If Norwell is not our guy, that is." He directed a pointed look to Odelia. "You're a pretty good judge of character, honey. How did the man strike you? Do you think he could be the guy we want for this?"

"I don't know, Uncle Alec. If he is, he's a pretty good actor. He really seemed heartbroken."

"He's heartbroken because Valina dumped him," said Chase. "That doesn't mean he didn't kill her out of spite."

"Unfortunately we don't have hard evidence to go after the guy," said Uncle Alec. "Only a lot of circumstantial stuff, which simply won't stand up in court." He sighed, then glanced down at me. "I never thought I'd say this, but how about you, little buddy? Any bright ideas? Cause now is a good time to share them with the rest of the team."

"I'm afraid I don't have anything for you at this time, Chief," I said. "Though you're probably right about Norwell Kulhanek. He does look very good for this: the man has motive, opportunity and means. In fact he's the perfect suspect. But no evidence."

Uncle Alec turned to Odelia, who shook her head. "He

likes Norwell for this, but as you say: as long as we don't have anything solid on the guy, we're totally stuck."

"Okay, people—not what I want to hear. So keep on digging and get me some results. Now get lost—all of you."

"What about the two couples in our holding cells?" asked Chase.

"Just let them go," said the Chief with a weary gesture of his hand. He thought for a moment, then added, "And let's pick up Norwell and give him the third-degree. See if we can't make the guy talk by leaning on him some."

"You mean now?"

"Nah, he can wait until tomorrow. Let's call it a night, folks."

CHAPTER 24

That evening, we found our friends disconsolate and glued to the couch.

"What's wrong?" I asked as I hopped up onto that same couch. Odelia had placed a blanket there, to protect the cushions from our sharp claws, and even though the blanket was nice enough, I must say I preferred the original. But then of course I could understand where she was coming from: nobody likes their cushion covers ripped up.

"Don't ask," said Harriet without even bothering to lift her head.

"Harriet has decided to quit cat choir," her mate announced, looking equally glum.

"Quit cat choir!" Dooley cried. "But why?!"

"Do you really have to ask?" said Harriet. "After last night's utter, complete disaster?"

"We went into town this morning," said Brutus, "and were met with snickers, whispers and funny faces wherever we went. We've officially turned into Hampton Cove's laughingstock. The butt of every joke. The focus of derision."

"I'm the laughingstock, Brutus," said Harriet. "Not you."

"I'm the laughingstock by association," Brutus clarified.

"I don't understand," I said. "All because of that Jack business?"

"Cats are mocking me, Max," Harriet said. "They're mocking me and calling me a funny old bird, with the emphasis on bird." She raised her voice, regaining some of the old Harriet fire. "The absolute worst thing you can call a cat is a bird, Max."

"They could call you a mouse," said Dooley. "That's probably just as bad. Or a chicken."

Harriet bridled. "Oh, Dooley, will you please shut up. I'm really not in the mood for your jokes."

"I wasn't joking," said Dooley, slightly taken aback by Harriet's outburst. "Kingman called Buster a chicken last week, when he said he was afraid to cross Main Street on account of all the traffic. Buster got upset and said he wasn't a chicken, and I told Kingman that Buster was right. He's a cat and not a chicken. Or is he?"

"No, Buster is definitely not a chicken," I assured my friend.

"See?" said Dooley. "That's what I told Kingman, but he just laughed and laughed and laughed."

"Oh, Dooley," said Harriet with a sigh, and replaced her head on her front paws.

Brutus drew me aside. "Did you get a chance to talk to Harriet about you-know-what?"

"Not yet," I said. "And I don't think now is a good time."

"No, I guess not," he said, darting an anxious glance at his lady love. "She's been like this all afternoon, and frankly I'm worried, Max. Cat choir has always been her thing. It's her life, you know, to be the star of the show. If you take that away from her, what does she have left?"

"Yeah, I know."

"Harriet needs to shine. Otherwise..." He gulped, afraid to utter the fateful words.

"So we'll simply have to convince her to go out there again, and ignore the gossipers."

"Easier said than done. You should have seen her this morning, Max. She was devastated. And gossip is such a hard thing to fight, you know. It's ephemeral."

I cast an admiring look at my friend. "Very perceptive," I said.

"I heard it from Marge. She used it to describe the general atmosphere in town right now. Said plenty of people have been gossiping behind her back, too. About Tex being on that list of cheaters."

"Yeah, but he explained that, didn't he?"

"I know, but who cares about the truth? People still talk, calling him a cheat, and Marge his poor victim, and freely speculating about their impending divorce."

"It will all die down soon enough," I said. "When the next big thing hits this town Valina Fawn and her site will be all but forgotten, and so will Tex's so-called infidelity."

"Even Odelia is having trouble. You should hear the kinds of things people are saying about her. Pregnant and with a cheat for a husband. It's not pretty, Max. Not pretty at all."

"But he wasn't even on the list. Someone simply used his name and likeness."

"Tell that to the gossipers. They're a hardy bunch. And they don't care about a silly little thing like the truth."

We both studied Harriet for a moment, then I said, "So maybe I'll have that chat now."

"You think that's a good idea?"

"It's not going to get any better, is it?"

"It's only going to get worse," he said resignedly.

"You better leave us, Brutus."

He gave me a grateful smile. "Thanks, Max. You're a true

friend. In fact," he added after a moment, "you and Dooley are probably the only friends we have—the rest are all backstabbers." And after expressing this harsh view, he slipped out through the pet flap and was gone.

So I took a deep breath and strode up to Harriet. After a silent whisper into Dooley's ear had dispatched him as well, it was just me and Harriet.

"It's a hard life, isn't it, Max?" she asked. "Tough, if you see what I mean."

"I'm sure it will all settle down soon enough," I said. "Cats are like people, Harriet. They like to latch onto the latest drama, but they also forget easily. Tomorrow there will be something new to gossip about, and your little predicament will be yesterday's news."

"I don't care. They said some nasty things behind my back, Max, and I've seen them for what they really are: a bunch of nasty gossips. You, Brutus and Dooley are the only true friends I have, and frankly I don't need anyone else. So from now on I won't stray past this house and the backyard, and that's fine by me. I'll be little miss homebody from now on. Queen of my own domain." She gave me a brave smile. "I'm sure I'll be perfectly happy."

"You won't be happy," I said. "You can't be happy unless you can shine. And in order to shine you need an audience. You know that, Harriet. You're a star, not a homebody."

"I am a star, aren't I?" she murmured. "A star without an audience. Because my audience has turned against me."

"They haven't turned against you. On the contrary. They think you handled that whole business with Jack with grace and poise and that *je-ne-sais-quoi* only a true star possesses."

She drew a tiny wrinkle across her brow. "You really think so?"

"Of course! Look, what is gossip other than admiration tinged with a touch of jealousy? These cats all admire you,

Harriet. I mean, who else but you has ever been serenaded by a bird, of all species! Who else inspires such unbridled devotion?"

"Keep going," she murmured, having closed her eyes as she took in these words.

"People don't just gossip about anyone, you know. They only gossip about the people they secretly or not-so-secretly envy. Deep down every cat in Hampton Cove looks up to you. They either aspire to be like you, or to be near you. It's the fate of every diva. Look at Meryl Streep, or Oprah Winfrey. Or even Beyoncé or Taylor Swift. The things people say about them—all because these people are the brightest stars on our firmament."

"Are you saying I'm such a star, Max?" she asked, her eyes brimming with tears now.

"That's exactly what I'm saying. You're Hampton Cove's biggest star, Harriet. And stars like you catch a lot of flak and attract ridicule. But they are also loved and admired by all."

"Oh, Max," she said, her chest heaving and falling rapidly. "Could you be right?"

"You know I'm right. Now go out there and shine, bright star. Light up that stage."

"Thank you, Max," she said fervently. "I guess I lost faith there for a moment. Faith in my own abilities. It's something that happens sometimes to us special ones, you know."

"I know, Harriet," I said with an encouraging smile. "Of course I know."

And I watched her glide to the floor with one graceful, fluid movement, then prance in the direction of the pet flap, her head held high, like a true feline princess, which she was. And she had just reached the pet flap when the flap flapped and a bird strutted through.

"Oh, Harriet!" he cried. "I've got another little poem prepared especially for you!"

And then Jack the sparrow, for of course it was he, settled down and started reciting his special little poem.

"Harriet, I love you.

Harriet my heart is true,

But my heart is also blue,

If you don't love me, too!"

But instead of getting upset, or breaking down into a flood of tears, this time Harriet simply inclined her head in a royal gesture, quietly murmured her gratitude for the bird's poem, and was on her way.

Your true star doesn't brush aside an earnest fan. They bask in the glow of their admiration, and use it as a stepping stone to ever greater heights of success and glory.

Jack, reeling after Harriet's response, now tottered back through the pet flap, and moments later could be heard singing a jubilant song from the top of the highest tree.

And since I was alone in the house, I decided to take another look at Pettr. And as I scrolled through the chats Harriet had engaged in, I saw that all of the pets that had written her were all fans, extending their admiration for her great talent. I smiled. So Harriet hadn't been cheating on Brutus after all. Instead she'd turned Pettr from a dating site into an admiration site. Her own personal fandom.

"Way to go, Harriet," I murmured as I put down the tablet.

Brutus had snuck back in, and I now informed him of my deductions. The smile that lit up his face was something to behold. He actually had tears in his eyes—tears of gratitude this time.

"I always knew being Harriet's partner wasn't going to be easy, Max," he said with a husky voice. "It's probably like being Meryl's husband, or Oprah's boyfriend. Her sheer star power is of such a magnitude that sometimes it's hard not to be overpowered."

"Always remember, Brutus," I said, "that a strong woman

needs a strong man. And I can tell you right now that you're exactly the kind of cat Harriet needs. In fact I can't think of a better partner for her than you, my good friend." I placed a solemn paw on his shoulder, and looked deep into his eyes. "You, my dear Brutus, complete her."

"Oh, Max," he said brokenly. And more tears were freely shed.

"Now go after her," I said. "Cause even though she'll never admit it, Harriet needs you, Brutus. In fact she needs you now more than ever."

He nodded wordlessly, then disappeared back through the pet flap.

I'd hopped onto the couch and was busy selecting the best spot when Dooley walked in. "What's going on, Max?" he asked. "First Harriet appeared, in tears, then Jack, in tears, and finally Brutus, also in tears. Why are you making everyone cry today?"

"Those were all tears of happiness, buddy," I said. "Tears of joy, not sorrow. And now if you'll excuse me, I think I've earned the right to take a long—very long nap."

And so I circled my spot three times, then languorously stretched myself out, and promptly dozed off.

CHAPTER 25

It had been a tough day, and Alec Lip was glad that it was finally over and he got to go home. Usually his home life sustained him, and provided the energy he needed to tackle another day at the office. But the last couple of days had thrown a wrench in the machinery, with Charlene suspecting him of tomfoolery with the Valina Fawn business. And even though she now seemed to believe that he had indeed created that profile for professional purposes and not personal ones, there was still a certain coolness between them, which grated on his sensitive soul.

He might look all tough and imposing, and as a cop didn't mind busting heads and cracking skulls, the fact of the matter was that he possessed a tender heart, and this recent frostiness in his one true love's manner was like a dark cloud that hung over him.

And he'd just decided to buy a bouquet of Charlene's favorite flowers—Mister Lincoln Roses—when he came upon his ma in the corridor. And as he approached, he could tell there was something seriously wrong with the woman. For she was smiling. Smiling like a maniac.

"What's wrong?" he asked immediately, his voice laced with earnest concern.

"Wrong? Nothing's wrong," said Vesta, still smiling that serial killer rictus.

"Your lips," said Alec. "They're all twisted up."

"What are you talking about! I'm trying to be nice!"

"You look like you're about to commit mass murder."

"Don't be an idiot. You told me to be nice to people. Scarlett told me to be nice to people. And now that I'm trying to be nice to people, you tell me I look like the Boston strangler! Well, thanks, Alec. Way to go."

He softened. "Being nice to people doesn't mean you have to grin like a lunatic, Ma. It just means you have to try to—"

"Put myself in their shoes. Yah, I got the lecture from Scarlett, thank you very much. And I'm trying, okay? In fact just now a woman called and said her husband fell down the stairs and I even congratulated her on a job well done."

"You did what?"

"I told her that I hoped she hadn't left any traces and that if she was careful she would probably get away with it. Us women have to look out for each other. If one of us shoves her husband down a flight of stairs because he's been treating her like dirt, it's important we show them the support and the respect they deserve."

He closed his eyes and slapped a hand to his weary brow.

And as they walked out together, she continued, "I asked her to check for a pulse, and she said she couldn't find one, and that she thought he'd broken his neck, so I told her good riddance and said I'd buy her dinner. Now tell me again I'm not being nice!"

"Dear God, give me strength," he muttered.

That night, as Alec and Charlene sat up in bed reading on their respective tablets, as they usually did—he a crime scene report and she the minutes of the latest Chamber of Commerce meeting—she suddenly lowered her tablet and took off her reading glasses.

"I haven't thanked you for those flowers yet."

"You're welcome," he muttered.

"Or the delicious dinner you cooked us."

"That's all right. No need to thank me."

She glanced over to her partner. "Alec?"

"Mh?"

"You're not still upset with me, are you?"

"Why would I be upset with you?"

"Because I thought you were cheating on me?"

This time he did look up, and gave her an inscrutable frown. "I thought I'd cleared that all up?"

"You did, and I'm glad you did, but the whole affair has left me wondering…"

"Yes?"

"There's something about me that you probably should now, darling."

He patiently waited until she'd elucidate, turning off his tablet.

"As you know, this isn't my first rodeo. And the person I was with at the time—Jim… Well, things between us didn't end well, let's just keep it at that. And it's made me… vulnerable, I guess you might say. Vulnerable and scared, maybe." She idly pulled at the strings of her nightie. "So when I saw your name appear on that list, I jumped to the conclusion…"

"I'm not Jim, Charlene," said Alec softly. And when she gazed up into his eyes, there was such gentleness there, and such understanding, that she felt her heart lurch.

"I know," she said, placing a hand on his jowly cheek. "And I'm sorry for doubting you."

"You don't have to apologize. If I saw your name on that list, I'd probably think the worst, too."

She pecked a tender kiss on his lips, and a warm glow spread through her chest. She was lucky to have met him, this rare specimen. And even though she still found it difficult sometimes to place her trust in him, it was getting a little easier every day, as she continued to chip away at the hard crust that had formed itself around her heart after the way Jim had treated her.

"My ma told me the most outrageous thing today," said Alec.

And as she settled in next to him, her head on his shoulder, she smiled and said, "What did she do this time?" Alec's mom was clearly certifiable, but the stories Alec told her about the old lady's crazy antics never failed to make her laugh.

The day dawned supreme, with a glorious sun peeping across the horizon the first chance she got, clearly as eager to start her new day as the rest of us. Though in all honesty just another hour of peace and quiet wouldn't have been unwelcome, if I'm honest. Cat choir had been an exuberant affair, with Harriet proudly reclaiming her position as queen of Hampton Cove, next to whom everyone else paled in comparison, Jack had once again sung from the highest tree and declared his love for Harriet to all and sundry, and Brutus strutted his stuff safe in the knowledge all was well with the world.

Seeking a cuddle and some attention, I snuck up on Odelia, while Dooley snuck up on Chase. Patiently we both waited until our humans stirred, and I now mewled quietly to draw their attention, then proceeded to burrow my nose into Odelia's armpit, even as Dooley burrowed his nose into Chase's. And so for the next ten minutes we all lay, the two of us purring with pleasurable abandon, and Odelia and Chase waking up to greet a new day.

You may wonder why I don't shudder at the smell of an unwashed armpit, but I have to admit I rather enjoy a rank body cavity. I guess human smells affect us differently. What humans find abhorrent, we consider perfectly yummy, and what they find delicious—those artificial scents sold in a bottle or cans of aerosolized deodorant—we find yucky.

Which just goes to show: excellence is in the nose of the beholder.

Odelia finally stirred and dislodged me. "Time to get up, buddy," she said, then yawned and stretched.

"Yeah, time to get up, Dooley," said Chase, and inspected his chest for puncture wounds. I admit that in the heat of the moment we do sometimes forget to retract our claws—call it a small token of our appreciation.

And so we watched as first Chase then Odelia stumbled out of bed, still sleep drunk, and headed into the bathroom for that first all-important business of the day: getting rid of any access fluids that may have accrued in their bladders overnight.

"Do you think today we'll finally catch Valina Fawn's murderer?" asked Dooley.

"Let's hope so," I said. "They are going to arrest Norwell Kulhanek, and if anyone can make that man break down it's Chase."

Just then, Chase's phone rang out its pleasant ringtone, Ed Sheeran's latest hit. He stepped out of the bathroom and hurried over. "Yello," he said with a frown. He then pressed a button and we could hear Gran's voice ringing through the room loud and clear.

"Yeah, another dead body," said the old lady. "This one seems to have slipped on a wine bottle and gotten the thing firmly lodged in its neck. So I told the person who called it in that it was probably just an accident, but she insisted it was murder. You can't argue with these people, Chase. They all got murder on the brain for some reason. I'm telling you—"

"Okay, so who's the dead guy?" asked Chase, cutting the flow of words.

"Guy called Norwell Kulhanek? Obviously an alcoholic, but what do I know. People keep telling me to be nice, and then when I'm being nice, they're still not happy. There really is no way of pleasing some people, is there? You know what the problem is? It's—"

"Where was this?" he asked curtly, ignoring Gran's outburst.

She gave him the address, and before she could launch into another stream of vituperation, he thanked her and hung up.

Odelia, who'd followed the conversation leaning against the doorpost, now nodded and burst into action, just as Chase did. Moments later they were both showered and dressed and we were on our way downstairs.

"Norwell Kulhanek, Max!" said Dooley. "Our main suspect!"

"I know. What are the odds?"

"Must be suicide. He killed Valina and felt the noose tightening around his neck and took the coward's way out."

"Let's just wait and see," I said, and braced myself for what we'd find.

CHAPTER 26

The co-owner of the Valina Fawn dating site was lying on his back surrounded by bottles of wine. We were in the basement of the Kulhanek place, which had been turned into a wine cellar. Racks had once been placed along the walls, but had been torn down, their contents now littered across the floor in a sea of broken bottles.

One of those bottles was still stuck in Norwell's neck, and it was hard to distinguish between wine and blood, as the two liquids had gotten mixed on the cement floor.

Abe Cornwall, who sat crouched over the body, now looked up. "Someone shoved a broken bottle into his carotid artery," he announced. "Causing him to bleed out. Death would have been pretty inevitable, and fairly quick."

"When did he die?" asked Chase as he surveyed the scene.

"Around eight last night I'd say. Anywhere between seven and nine will do."

"Do you think this could have been an accident?" asked Odelia. "Knocked over a rack of bottles and one of them ended up in his neck?"

"Doubtful," said Abe, shaking his head. "Though not

impossible. If he'd had the misfortune to land on top of a broken bottle, it might have penetrated the artery. Though I'd have to say chances of that happening are pretty slim." He got up out of his crouch. "And then of course there's this." He held up a plush Cupid doll with his gloved hand. The doll had either wine or blood on it. "Found on top of the victim's body. He could have been clutching it in his arms when he fell, of course, but somehow I doubt it." And he handed the plush doll to Chase, who'd also donned plastic gloves for the occasion.

Even Dooley and I were donning plastic booties—just as a precaution.

Chase and Odelia studied the doll together. "It's the same one, all right," was Odelia's determination.

"Same what?" asked Abe.

"Valina Fawn. The doll is used as her site's logo," Chase explained. "Same one was found on Valina's body."

"Oh, that's right. I remember now," said the coroner. "Well, that probably cinches it. Though it still doesn't explain who dun it." He gave Chase a wink. "But I'm sure you'll figure that out for us. That's why they pay you the big bucks, after all."

"Yeah, right," Chase grunted as he handed the Cupid doll back and Abe stuffed it into a plastic evidence bag.

We mounted the wooden stairs and soon arrived in the kitchen, where Emma Kulhanek was sitting at the kitchen table, sipping from a cup of tea, and being consoled by a woman officer. When we arrived, the officer rose from her chair and left the room.

"Is he... all right?" asked Emma, her teary face displaying a glimmer of hope.

"I'm afraid not," said Odelia. "Not much we can do for him."

"Oh, God," said Emma, and broke down again.

"I'm sorry to do this, Emma," said Chase, "but we're going to have to ask you a couple of questions, if that's all right."

She nodded, and pressed a wad of tissues to her runny nose.

"Was it you who found Norwell?" asked Odelia, taking a seat at the kitchen table.

"I wondered where he was when I woke up," said Emma. "We had a big row yesterday, after I found out about him and... well, you know."

Odelia placed a comforting hand on the woman's arm.

"So I told him he could sleep on the couch, until I decided what I was going to do. I was thinking about taking the kids to my parents, but they love their dad, and I don't like to interrupt their regular routine. But this morning when I came downstairs, he wasn't on the couch, and so I figured he'd already left for work. But then when I headed out myself, I saw his car was still in the garage, so that's when I realized that something was wrong."

"Where are the kids now?" asked Odelia, concern lacing her voice.

"School. I dropped them off with my parents yesterday after school, and they took them in this morning. I didn't want the kids to be here when Norwell and I... talked things through. I had a feeling it might get messy, and they didn't need to hear all that." She took a breath, trying to compose herself. "So I tried to reach him on his phone, but he didn't pick up, until I heard his ringtone somewhere close by. So I kept on ringing him, and that's when I found him, lying there, surrounded by all those bottles! He-he must have gone down there to get a bottle, and fallen over and dragged down all of those bottle racks."

"You didn't hear anything last night? Those falling bottles must have made a lot of noise," said Chase.

"I wasn't here last night. Parent-teacher night. I only got in around ten and went straight to bed. The last thing I needed was another confrontation with Norwell."

"You didn't notice him missing?"

She shook her head. "I went straight upstairs. I was still very much upset."

"Parent-teacher night started at what time, exactly?" asked Chase.

"Seven. But I got there early, to set up the room and get ready."

"Thank you, Emma," said Odelia. "You did well."

"Those bottles..." said Chase.

"Norwell's hobby. He loved his wine. Even thought about buying his own vineyard in Napa Valley. We were always going on wine tours when we were still living in San Francisco. Though of course they probably have some excellent wines out here, too." Her face seemed to crumple like a used tissue, and moments later she was crying again.

"Tough," said Dooley once we had left the kitchen and wandered out into the backyard to get some fresh air. "First she discovers that her husband was having an affair, and now he's dead. Do you think he was murdered, Max?"

"It certainly looks that way," I said.

"First Valina Fawn, and now her business partner. So both of the site's owners have been murdered, and probably by the same killer, wouldn't you say?"

"The presence of that Cupid doll certainly points to the same person."

"And our favorite suspect as well. Looks like we'll have to start from scratch."

"Yup. Back to square one," I said, and we both settled in and watched police officers, crime scene people and all the hullaballoo involved in a murder investigation gain momentum. Hopefully all that activity would provide a telling clue. A fingerprint, a DNA sample, a footprint—anything that would lead us to a killer who'd already murdered twice, and so far with absolute impunity.

CHAPTER 27

We'd just settled in for the duration, when Chase walked into the backyard. He was talking into his phone and had the excited look on his face of a man who's made a big discovery. Kids on Christmas morning have that same look, or geeks about to meet their favorite *Star Wars* actor at their local comic-con.

"That's great!" he said to the person on the other end. "Send a unit there immediately. Yeah, I'm on my way." He tucked his phone into his pocket, then turned to us. "Let's go," he said, and when we didn't immediately spring into action, he simply slipped two large hands under our respective midsections and lifted us clear into the air!

He practically ran into the house and when he came upon Odelia, still sitting with a distraught-looking Emma Kulhanek, he said, "There's been a development, babe. We have to go." And still carrying us, he hurried out of the house, then to his car. For a moment he didn't know what to do—you can't use your car keys when you're holding two cats—and then found nothing better than to deposit us both on top of the car!

"I just hope he won't forget us and drive off," I muttered.

"He won't," Dooley assured me. "Chase is always very careful, and so is Odelia."

So we patiently waited until one or the other would take us down, but suddenly we heard two doors slam shut and moments later the car lurched into motion!

"Hang on, Dooley!" I cried. "Looks like they have forgotten about us!"

Luckily, the roof of Chase's car has iron bars, in case he has to transport a whole gang of criminals at once, I guess, and so we managed to hold onto those while the pickup raced through traffic at breakneck speed, Chase not even bothering to stop at intersections or respect red lights!

"This whine is terrible!" I yelled to my friend, referring to the police siren.

"What wine!" asked Dooley.

"Not wine, the whine—the noise!"

"Oh, I thought that was you, Max!" Dooley said.

When people refer to the view from the top, I never thought this was it. Somehow I'd always imagined it as something magical, wonderful and exhilarating. I can tell you it certainly was exhilarating, but definitely not a lot of fun!

We saw the world sort of swoosh by, people and houses and cars a kind of blur, though that could have been my eyes watering up from the wind, of course. And then there were the flies hitting me in the face when I least expected it, and at least one big bumblebee. Lucky for the bee—and me—it wasn't hurt in the collision, and after grumbling something that didn't sound very nice, it simply flew on.

Finally we arrived at our destination, which was a house in the suburbs, and Chase braked so hard and so suddenly that we actually slid from the roof and down the windshield. And I know you think cats are all-purpose pets, but using us as windshield wipers is taking things a little too far in my estimation.

The good thing was that as we slipped down the windshield, making a sort of squeaky sound, we got a first-row seat to watch Odelia and Chase's twin expressions of horror.

"Oh, my God, Chase!" Odelia cried. "We forgot about the cats!"

"Sorry, babe," the cop grunted, then got out and subjected us to a brief inspection. "They look fine," he finally determined, and promptly lost interest in our precarious fate.

Lucky for us Odelia is a more responsible pet parent, and took more time to make sure we were all right, and hadn't been harmed in the taping of this sequence. We could always have lodged a formal complaint with American Humane, of course, but Odelia was right: we might both be shaken—or even stirred—but we were fundamentally fine.

More police cars arrived, and soon a kind of impressive police presence built up in front of that inoffensive house in the suburbs.

"What's going on?" I asked. "Why are we here?"

"One of Chase's officers has found a name that appears on both the Valina Fawn membership list and the Brookwell membership list," Odelia explained. "A person named Alec March, who has a criminal record and looks like our most promising suspect yet."

"A criminal record for what?" I asked as I flicked one final fly from my corpus.

"Murder," said Odelia with a touch of ominousness.

Suddenly a voice from inside the house shouted, "Don't come any closer—I have a hostage and I will not hesitate to shoot!" And to show us he meant what he said, Alec March—for I assumed it was him—squeezed off a shot.

Immediately the officers present all ducked down behind

their squad cars, and the siege—or hostage situation—was now well underway.

"I wonder who the hostage is, Max," said Dooley, like me hiding next to the car's wheel. But as we glanced over, the man of the hour briefly appeared in the window, a gun pressed to a woman's head, and as we got a good look at the both of them, we gasped in shock. For in that brief moment I'd recognized the hostage as... Ida Baumgartner!

"It's Ida," I heard Odelia say.

Ida Baumgartner is one of Tex's most loyal patients, never shy of coming up with a new disease she's suffering from. She's very big on Dr. Google and can invent a new disease every day of the week and twice on Sunday. The woman has survived all the different cancers known to man, heart atrophy, dengue fever, malaria, herpes...

"Looks like Ida has finally met her match," said Dooley. "A disease that might prove incurable."

"I'm not sure prisoners' rights activists or their spokesperson Kim Kardashian would approve of referring to an ex-convict as a disease, Dooley," I said, "but I'm afraid you're right. This is not a malady that can be fixed by popping a pill or sticking on a band-aid."

"Heeeeelp!" now Ida cried. "This man has a gun!"

That much was already obvious, of course.

"I came here for a date and he suddenly pulled a gun on me!"

Now this was news to all of us.

"Ida is here on a date?" I asked.

"She must have created a profile on Pettr," said Dooley.

"Pettr is strictly for pets, Dooley," I said. "It's far more likely she created a profile on Valina Fawn and made a match with our Alec March."

"I wonder how that algorithm works, Max. To match a

known murderer with a hypochondriac like Ida Baumgartner."

"I have no idea." We could have asked Norwell, who created part of the algorithm, but since the man was now lying dead amongst his wine bottles that would be a hard ask. "Maybe hypochondria and homicidal ideation share certain traits?" I suggested.

"So do you think all murderers are hypochondriacs?"

"Doubtful," I said. "Though hypochondria could lead to murder, when a hypochondriac doesn't find a receptive doctor to listen to their concerns and decides to shoot them."

"Heeeeeeelp meeeeeeeeee!" Ida was bellowing.

"Oh, shut up!" her attacker cried.

I could see the man, and thought that he didn't look like much. He sported a shaved head, several scars on his face, and a large swastika tattoo on his neck. Not exactly Ida's dream lover I should have thought. Then again, Photoshop is the online dater's friend.

"Drop your weapon and come out now!" Chase shouted.

"No way!" the man returned.

"You're completely surrounded, Alec! No escape!"

"I want a helicopter, a private plane fueled and ready at JFK and five million dollars in unmarked bills! You've got one hour, cop, or I start shooting hostages!"

This caused a ripple of concern to travel through the collected cop contingent.

"Hostages?" I heard Chase ask. "I thought he had just the one?"

But I now saw that a small doggie had appeared in the window. It was Ida Baumgartner's long-haired teacup Chihuahua Minnie Mouse, and she looked nervous and not a little bit scared.

"He's going to shoot the dog, Max!" said Dooley. "The man is a maniac!"

"He's certainly something else," I agreed.

"We have to do something. We have to save that dog!"

So you see, cats have this reputation for disliking and even taunting dogs, but when push comes to shove, we are willing to put our lives on the line for the species!

Uncle Alec now also arrived, and he had brought a gift in the form of Gran.

"What's going on?" asked the Chief.

"This guy Alec March is threatening to start shooting hostages when he doesn't get what he wants," said Chase.

Uncle Alec grabbed a bullhorn from his car and raised it to his lips. "Alec March, this is Chief Alec Lip. Release those hostages now and I promise we won't hurt you!"

"Buzz off, Alec!" shouted Alec, then put the muzzle of his gun to the little doggie's head!

It whimpered and shook and the scene broke my heart.

"Oh, enough of this," suddenly said Gran. "No more Miss Nice Gal!" she yelled, and before anyone could stop her, she had grabbed that bullhorn and now strode to the fore. "You stop this nonsense right now, Alec March!" she bellowed, her voice amplified and echoing between the houses. "If you dare to harm a hair on that poor creature's head, I'm going to personally come up there and whoop your ass, young man!"

"Go away, granny!" the hoodlum returned.

"Don't you granny me!" Gran boomed. "Drop your weapon and come out with your hands in the air. And don't make me come in there!"

"Go to hell!"

"You had your chance. It's whooping time!"

"Gran, no!" Odelia yelled.

But the old lady had dropped the bullhorn and now broke into a run, heading for the window. And as the man saw her coming, he raised his gun and aimed it straight at her head.

"Don't you dare!" Gran yelled. "Ida, conk him on his fat head!"

I could tell that Ida hadn't responded well to the situation. First to discover that her prince charming is actually an ogre, and then to have that ogre point a gun at her precious darling, her sweet treasure Minnie Mouse, it was clear she was seething with righteous anger. So the moment Mr. March turned the gun in Gran's direction, Ida didn't waste time lallygagging but picked up the first object she could find, which was a large vase that had been languishing on the windowsill, and crashed it down on top of the man's head.

For a moment the career criminal stood there, swaying in the breeze like a young sapling experiencing its first storm, and then he fell to earth and knew no more.

"Well done," said Gran, congratulating the other woman.

"Oh, dear," said Ida, pressing her precious darling to her sizable bosom. "I really thought I was a goner this time, Vesta. If it hadn't been for you, I don't know what I would have done!"

"You could have told him about your many incurable diseases," Gran suggested kindly as she inspected the unconscious man. "Scared the living daylights out of him."

"Always the joker, aren't you," said Ida tersely. "Such a wonderful sense of humor."

About a thousand cops converged on the scene now, and if Mr. March had still been conscious he would have been read his rights in no time. Now they had to wait for an ambulance to arrive and make sure he would live to enjoy a renewed sojourn in the pen.

"Got him!" said Chase jubilantly.

"Good job," said Odelia, addressing her grandmother.

"If you pull another stunt like that," said Uncle Alec, "you're grounded."

"You can't ground me," said Gran. "I'm your mother!"

"Watch me," Uncle Alec growled. "You almost gave me a heart attack when you stormed forward like that!"

"I learned that from Mel," said Gran with a smile.

"Who's Mel?" asked Chase.

"*Braveheart*!"

"Didn't Mel die in that movie?" asked Odelia.

"Poppycock," said Gran. "True heroes never die. Oh, and now for the reason I came down here in the first place. I quit."

"Quit?" asked Uncle Alec. "What do you mean you quit?"

"A man just called me a very bad name, and I came here to tell you that I'm too old to take that kind of abuse, so I quit."

"What did you do?"

"Why does everyone immediately assume it's my fault!" But when Uncle Alec fixed her with a steady look, she finally admitted, "Okay, so maybe I told him that he should put his head in a toilet and flush. But only because he was drunk and abusive!"

"Oh, Ma," said Uncle Alec with a sigh.

"He told me I was off my rocker!"

Uncle Alec hoisted up his pants. "I accept your resignation," he said, and he actually smiled as he spoke these words. "You are hereby relieved of your duties. Happy now?"

"You certainly look happy," Gran grumbled.

"That's because we just caught the person responsible for two murders." And to show us how grateful he actually was, he shook Odelia's hand, then Chase's hand, and practically went skipping back to his car, overall the picture of a happy chief of police.

CHAPTER 28

I have to say that even though the investigation was concluded—and with a neat bow tied on top, no less—I still didn't feel entirely satisfied with the way it had been wrapped up. Now you could ascribe this to the fact that I hadn't been instrumental in nabbing the killer, and you would be mistaken. It really doesn't matter to me who catches the bad guy—I'm not peacockish that way, or even wrapped up in my own sense of self-importance.

No, the thing was that Alec March being billed as Valina Fawn and Norwell Kulhanek's killer simply didn't seem to fit. For one thing, how had the man managed to get a hold of Norwell's key card? Though of course he could have gained access to the office at some point during the day, or bumped into Norwell at a coffee shop or gas station. I'm sure the investigation would bear all this out.

Still, I had a strong sense of unease, which drove me to pay a visit to Kingman, which is usually where my paws take me when I'm in a quandary.

Dooley accompanied me into town, and soon we found ourselves outside the General Store, where our voluminous piebald friend was sunning himself in front of his human's popular store.

"Hiya, fellas," said Kingman. "Phew, this sun is something else today, isn't it?" He got up lazily. "In fact I think I'm going to lie in the shade for a while. It's definitely getting too hot for my taste."

"Too much sun is bad for your skin," said Dooley. "It can even cause skin cancer."

Kingman gave him a strange look. "Cats are covered in fur, Dooley. The sun can't even reach our skin. So I don't think we're in any danger there."

"The sun can still reach our ears, Kingman. And our nose. And paw pads. And it's exactly those spots that are in grave danger of being affected by the sun's death rays."

Kingman offered me a grin. "Death rays. You'd think this is an episode of *Star Trek*."

"But it's true!" Dooley insisted. "I saw a documentary the other night that said that cats and dogs should watch out for their nekkid bits. Or put sunblock on them."

"Imagine that," said Kingman, still gripped by his bout of mirth. "Me asking Wilbur to rub sunblock all over my nekkid bits."

"Well, he should," said Dooley. "At least if he's a responsible pet daddy."

"Pet daddy," Kingman laughed. "Dooley, you should really consider doing standup."

"I am standing up," said Dooley.

"I know you are, buddy," said Kingman. "Better take a load off your paws and take a break. I hear you caught that nasty killer?"

"You heard about that?" I said, much surprised.

"Hey, news travels fast in this town. I heard it from Buster, who heard it from one of Fido's clients, who got it from the horse's mouth—in this case Ida Baumgartner herself."

"Yeah, Ida was in some real danger back there," I murmured, as I thought back to those moments fraught with mortal tension.

"So why aren't you smiling?" asked Kingman. "The bad guy is caught. Three rousing cheers for the good guys, right?"

"Max isn't sure we got the right bad guy," said Dooley.

"I've got this feeling," I said.

"Uh-oh," said Kingman. "I know all about that, buddy."

"You do?"

"Oh, absolutely. It's like when I dated this girl Eleanor, you know. She was perfect in every possible way. Great legs, cute face, amazing tail, but I don't know. Something just didn't seem to click. And for the life of me, I just couldn't figure out what it was. Until she dumped me for Tigger—the plumber's cat, and then I knew."

"What did you know?" I asked.

"I just told you. She dumped me for the plumber's cat. That's what was wrong with her."

"But... you couldn't have known that, could you?"

"I must have sensed it. And also, she kept asking me about Tigger. So now I figure she used me to get to know Tigger, and once she got her first introduction, she jumped at the chance, if you see what I mean."

"Are Eleanor and Tigger still together?" asked Dooley, who's a romantic at heart.

"Nah. Tigger introduced her to Shadow, and so she dumped Tigger and hooked up with Shadow. Then Shadow introduced her to his buddy Tom, and... Well, I guess you know what happened next."

"Where is Eleanor now?" asked Dooley.

"No idea. She skipped town a while back. Guess she ran out of potential hookups." He frowned and directed a look of concern at me. "Are you all right there, buddy? You look like you've seen a ghost."

"The ghost of Eleanor," Dooley quipped.

"No, it's just…" I said, squinting hard.

"Oh, I see what's going on," said Kingman. "You got one of your brainwaves, haven't you?"

I nodded quietly. I did have a brainwave. Or at least something had clicked, though I still didn't fully understand what, or why—or even who. But Kingman's words had definitely brought back a vague memory of… something. But what was it, exactly?

And as I settled down next to my friends, and Kingman and Dooley continued chatting amiably, suddenly the truth hit me.

"Of course," I murmured. "Why didn't I see it sooner!"

CHAPTER 29

I have to say it wasn't exactly my finest hour, or at least it didn't feel that way. It should have been, of course, for I'd finally cracked the case—figured out who had killed two people in cold blood. But instead of feeling the exhilaration when the arrest of a killer is finally within reach, I felt a little sad. For this time the killer was a person I liked.

Odelia and Chase leaned against the hood of the car, with Dooley and myself at their feet. Odelia had asked me more than once already how I thought this would go, and frankly I had no idea. I didn't think there would be a lot of resistance, though, or even any trickery needed to force a confession.

And I was right.

Emma Kulhanek walked out of the school entrance, spotted us and seemed to collapse into herself. And when Chase approached her and told her she was under arrest for the murders of Valina Fawn and Norwell Kulhanek, she simply bowed her head and nodded.

"I'm glad it's all over," she said quietly as she held out her hands.

"I'm not going to cuff you in front of your students, Emma," said Chase.

"Thank you," said the teacher. "That's very kind of you, detective." She paused and glanced back to the school. "What's going to happen to my kids now?"

"We spoke to your parents," said Odelia. "Asked them to pick them up."

Emma nodded and quite willingly got into the car.

At the police station she didn't sit in an interview room, but simply in Chase's office, which was a lot nicer than the formal interview rooms, and as she held a cup of tea between both hands, started to talk without even being prompted. It really was as if she wanted to get it off her chest, which I could absolutely understand. Committing murder creates a burden on one's soul, especially for a, essentially kindhearted person like Emma.

"I never wanted to come to Hampton Cove in the first place," she said. "It was Norwell's idea. He had heard about Valina's new site and thought if he could get in at the beginning, it might be a way for him to generate a lot of money, really launch his career, you know. He knew, of course, that Valina and I had been in school together, and badgered me into making the necessary introductions. He then used the fact that my family was still here, and that our kids could go to the same school I'd gone to to pressure me into agreeing to the big move back east. I finally relented, figuring that maybe he was right."

"But he wasn't," said Odelia softly. "Because you hadn't told him about Valina."

Emma took a deep breath. "Valina wasn't the sweet person everyone thought she was. She was a bully, and terrorized me mercilessly all through high school. Every single day she used to be on my case, and I hated her for it. She made my life a living hell, for six long years. So when I finally met her again, I somehow expected her to apologize. But she wouldn't even acknowledge what she'd done to me, much less show the least regret."

"And then your husband started an affair with her."

"I met a boy in the sixth grade. He was my first boyfriend. He was kind and warm and funny, and he defended me against Valina and her friends. I was in love with him, and thought things were finally going to change. So Valina, when she saw how happy I suddenly was, decided to steal him away from me. And she did. And then once she'd got her claws in him she made him dump me in front of the whole school, humiliating me even further. And so when she had the opportunity to go after Norwell, she didn't hesitate. She even had the gall to rub my face in it. When the list leaked she called to tell me about Norwell's affair. Said it didn't mean anything. Just a fling. For her it probably was, but not for Norwell. He was absolutely smitten. She had that effect on people. She could be very charming if she wanted to, but also completely ruthless. So when Norwell kept sending her messages and begging her to get back together, she found it amusing. Said he followed her around like a lapdog. Asked if it didn't bring back memories. Of course it did. Bullies never change. Not really. Unless you put them in their place. Only I should have done it twenty years ago, then things wouldn't be such a mess now."

"I'm sorry," said Odelia. "I didn't know."

"Nobody knew, except me and Valina, and of course the clique she used to hang out with back then. Her executioners. I hadn't even told Norwell, or my parents." She bowed her head. "She shouldn't have gone after Norwell. That was probably what drove me to... well, you know."

"You took his key card?" asked Chase.

"It was easy. In and out like a flash. I was afraid someone would see me, but nobody did. I didn't even try to hide or cover my tracks. At that point I was beyond caring." She took a thoughtful sip from her cup. "I used to do some shooting back in the day, and Norwell had a bow and arrows lying around, from the club. It just seemed appropriate. With her always pretending to be Cupid, while in actual fact she was just a monster."

"And then you dropped Norwell's key card on Meghan's desk."

"Yes. And I honestly thought that would be the end of it. With my tormentor finally dead, I thought I would be able to breathe again—to be free at least. But Norwell kept pining for her. He didn't have to say it, but I could feel it. He was still in love with the woman, in spite of everything she had done to me. So I finally broke down and told him. All of it. The bullying, the boyfriend she stole from me—the reason I moved to the other side of the country, away from my friends, my family—simply to be as far away from her as possible. And you know what he said? That he didn't believe me. That I was making it all up out of sheer spite. And that if he could, he would have left me for Valina."

"And so you decided to kill him, too," said Odelia.

"I didn't really decide anything. I was simply so fed up... I'd forgotten my laptop at home, so I slipped out of the parent-teacher meeting to quickly fetch it, making sure nobody saw me, since it's frowned upon to just disappear like that. I found Norwell in the basement, dusting off his cherished bottles, which he probably cared for more than me or the kids. He was crying, said he missed her so much. Said I couldn't understand what she had meant to him. As if she was the love of his life or something. I got so angry, so I just broke one of his precious bottles, just to get back at him. And when he lunged at me, in a reflex action I held it out to defend myself. It accidentally hit him in the neck, and before I knew what was happening, he was lying there, bleeding out. And I should have felt pity, or remorse, or regret, but all I felt was satisfaction and relief. In the end he had let me down. Me and the kids. So I wiped my prints, dropped the bottle, tore down those bottle racks to make it look as if someone had ransacked the place, and walked out."

"And returned to the school."

"Nobody had even noticed I was gone. It was so easy, just like with Valina. As if I was invisible." She looked up. "So how did you figure it out?"

"We talked to some of the parents. They did notice that you were gone for a while, Emma. And once we knew that, we checked traffic cameras along the route you took, and tracked your movements. It wasn't difficult to pinpoint the exact time you passed."

"I'm not sorry I killed them, you know," said Emma. "The only thing I'm sorry about is that my kids will grow up knowing their mom killed their dad. And my parents, of course. They'll be devastated."

And as Chase led her away, Odelia heaved a deep sigh. "Good work, Max," she said. "Too bad it was Emma. She was the last person I'd expected."

"It's something Kingman said that triggered a memory," I said. "Or several ones, actually. Emma once told us something about a bullying campaign she was very passionate about, explaining that it was a campaign close to her heart. And then there was the fact that she and Valina had gone to the same school together. She also mentioned during a book club meeting that she'd once been betrayed by a boyfriend who left her for another woman, and somehow all those elements suddenly clicked. And of course when you look back, it was always obvious that it must have been her: she would be the most obvious person to have access to her husband's key card, or his archery club gear, and we knew that her husband had been having an affair with Valina."

"Yeah, it all seems obvious now," said Odelia. "But it certainly wasn't obvious before."

"Poor woman," said Dooley. "Bullying is a terrible thing, isn't it, Odelia?"

"Oh, yeah. It can really traumatize a person for life. With terrible consequences."

Chase had returned and took a seat behind his desk. "Right," he said. "And now for the paperwork..."

In a few words, Odelia related to the cop what I'd told her.

He rubbed his nose. "I better not put that in my report. The DA might frown upon the testimony of a cat, though the defense will have a field day and might even be able to get the jury to let Emma off with a suspended sentence."

"I doubt it," said Odelia. "She did confess."

"Yes, she did." He smiled at me. "Good job, Max. You made us all look good again. And now if you'll excuse me, folks, looks like I'll be here all night, writing this all down!"

CHAPTER 30

Tex had fired up the grill, and delicious smells were wafting from the contraption and making our mouths water. It's too much to say that the man is a skilled grill master, but lately he has been proficient in not destroying what is supposed to be a feast for the taste buds and an excuse for the whole family to get together and enjoy each other's company.

"So are you still the dispatcher *du jour*, Vesta?" asked Charlene.

"No, I quit," said Gran as she ladled potato salad onto the Mayor's plate. "Couldn't handle the abuse anymore. You wouldn't believe how ungrateful some people are."

"I can imagine," said Charlene with a glance to Chief Alec.

"How about you, Scarlett?" asked Marge. "Are you still in the saddle?"

"No," said Scarlett. "Dolores finally returned, and so my services are no longer required." She sounded a little peeved about this, but then that's the fate of a temp: once the titular dispatcher returns to the position, the replacement is thanked for services rendered. "I thoroughly enjoyed it, though," said Scarlett. "An invaluable experience."

"A thankless experience, you mean," said Gran.

"Now, what did we say about being nice, Vesta?" said Scarlett.

Immediately Gran spirited a sort of weird grin onto her face.

"Please don't do that, Ma," said Uncle Alec. "You're going to scare the kids."

"What kids? We don't have no kids here."

"Soon," said Odelia with a warm smile. "Very soon."

"Have you started Lamaze yet?" asked Scarlett. "You really have to get in early. I hear these classes can be very popular and book out months in advance."

"Oh, and don't forget about booking your kid into a good primary school," said Charlene. "They should be starting to take admissions soon."

"And high school," Gran pointed out. "You can't apply too soon."

"And what about university?" Chase asked with a slow grin.

"It's no laughing matter, mister," said Charlene. "All the best places fill up fast, and if you don't get in there first, your little one will miss an important opportunity."

But Odelia didn't look overly concerned about the possibility of missing out on signing her future baby up for college. She took all these recommendations in stride, and so did Chase. And in doing so, they cemented my conviction that they would probably make great parents to the little one.

"Who's Lamaze?" asked Dooley.

"It's a series of breathing exercises to give pain relief to the expectant mother," I said.

"Pain relief! What do you mean!"

"Having a baby is not a walk in the park, Dooley," said

Harriet. "It does involve a certain degree of stress for the human body."

"Nothing Odelia can't handle," said Brutus with the absolute conviction of a cat who's never had babies and never will.

"Do you think Odelia might... die!" Dooley demanded.

"It does happen that women die in labor," Harriet admitted.

"Oh, no!" Dooley cried, jumping up from his seat on the porch and making it swing so powerfully that we all fell off. "Odelia!" he bellowed. "Stop this now! It's too dangerous!"

The humans all looked up at the commotion Dooley's screams had caused.

"What's eating sweet little Dooley?" asked Scarlett curiously.

"He's concerned about my health," said Odelia as Dooley jumped up onto her lap. She gave him a gentle cuddle. "It's all right, Dooley," she said. "I'll be fine."

"But Harriet just said that people who have babies all die!"

Odelia directed a censorious look in Harriet's direction, who shrugged it off with customary disdain. "I'll be perfectly safe," she assured our friend. "Isn't that true, Dad?"

Tex looked up from his grill. He'd been glued to the contraption, afraid lest he allow the sausages to burn, as he often did. The man was absentminded to a degree, and therefore probably not the best person to be allowed near food prep. "Mh?" he said.

"Can you explain to Dooley that nowadays having a baby poses very little risk to mother and child?"

"Oh, absolutely," said Tex. "You see, Dooley, our hospitals are so well-equipped to handle childbirth that we have managed to reduce the risk considerably. In fact in this country you're probably more at risk at dying from a plant dropping on top of your head as you walk down the street than in childbirth." And to illustrate his statement, he started rattling off a series of statistics, gesticulating wildly with his tongs to prove his point.

"Tex, the sausages!" suddenly Marge cried.

Black smoke was wafting up from the grill, and Tex uttered a strangled cry.

America as a civilized nation might have succeeded in considerably lowering maternal mortality with the assistance of good doctors like Tex, but this apparently didn't extend to the death of innocent sausages on the grill.

Lucky for us, Marge produced a fresh set of pristine sausages from a secret hiding place, and Chase took over from a disappointed Tex.

"My plan B," Marge said with a wink, long association with her husband having made her an expert on all things Tex Poole.

And so before long we were all tucking in, even Tex, who had to admit that his son-in-law made an excellent cook.

The only one who didn't look convinced was Dooley, but then Dooley tends to fret. I guess that's what makes him Dooley, and why we all love him so much.

And we'd all settled down and were enjoying the pleasant family gathering, when all of a sudden a loud singing sounded from a nearby tree.

"Harriet, lovely Harriet!" the voice caroled.

"Oh, God, not again!" Brutus cried.

For it was indeed Jack the sparrow, who had returned to try his luck in love and fight for Harriet's heart once and for all.

"I'll duel you for her, cat!" Jack now said, adopting a pugilistic stance and demonstrating some dazzling footwork. "You and me—may the best man win!"

"I'm not dueling you, bird," said Brutus.

"Right here, right now!" said Jack, flying down from his

perch and walking up to Brutus. "I'm throwing down the gauntlet! Pick it up if you dare!"

"He does have guts, doesn't he?" I said.

"Or a death wish," said Harriet without much excitement. She might like her suitors, but this bird definitely did not set her soul on fire.

"Look, Jack," said Brutus. "I don't want to fight you. So just buzz off, will you?"

"I'll even let you throw the first punch!" said Jack, and offered his right cheek.

"What's that bird doing?" asked Scarlett.

"Trying to engage Brutus in a fight for Harriet's hand," Gran explained.

Jack now hauled off and gave Brutus a light kick against the paw. "Take that, cat!" he said. "And that!"

"Oh, for goodness sakes..." Brutus muttered, and placed his paw squarely on top of the bird, completely hiding him from view.

In spite of this harsh treatment, we could still hear Jack cry, "You can't beat me, cat! I'm Jack the sparrow and I'm not afraid of no stinkin' cat!"

"Just leave him be, Brutus," I said.

"He's so annoying," Brutus sighed, and removed his paw again.

Jack spent a few seconds catching his breath, then finally sank down onto his haunches, looking a little spent. "Okay, so you won this round. But the next one is mine."

"Sure thing, bird," said Brutus magnanimously, then pushed some sausage in the sparrow's direction. "Care for a piece?"

Jack eyed it for a moment with suspicion, then relented. "Don't mind if I do," he said.

Moments later cat and bird were sharing a meal in companionable silence.

"This is some pretty good stuff," said Jack finally.

"Isn't it?" said Brutus.

"You know, for a cat you ain't half bad."

"Thanks. For a bird I guess you're okay."

Hampton Cove, people. Probably the only place on the planet where cats and birds can live in peace. Then again, why wouldn't they? Brutus and Jack had a lot in common after all: an abiding affection for a certain capricious female feline.

More fascinating conversation was probably enjoyed by all, but at that moment sleep overtook me. Can you blame me? All this running around had seriously cut into my nap time and I needed to catch up. So I decided to get my napping in while the napping was good.

And I'd just drifted off when suddenly Dooley piped up.

"Max?"

"Mh?"

"So about that man's hairy ass—"

"Dooley!"

THE END

Thanks for reading! If you want to know when a new Nic Saint book comes out, sign up for Nic's mailing list: nicsaint.com/news

EXCERPT FROM PURRFECT HIT (MAX 48)

Chapter One

As you may or not know, cats are creatures of habit. And for the longest time it has been my habit and Dooley's to spend part of the night in peaceful repose at the foot of our human's bed. But recently Odelia has started sleeping restlessly, tossing and turning and generally making a nuisance of herself and preventing us from getting any sleep.

According to her it's something to do with this minor experience she's going through called pregnancy, which is probably simply an excuse to create trouble for us, for how can something like a baby kicking away against her tummy and her body blowing up like a balloon cause her any kind of inconvenience? I am, of course, joking. I totally understand how sleep has become an elusive proposition for her, and therefore also for us.

And since Gran was away on holiday—she and her best friend Scarlett had signed up for a Norwegian cruise, thinking Norway is a tropical destination in the Caribbean while in actual fact it's probably one of your more frosty destinations you can pick out of the cruise vacation arsenal—we'd been sleeping on Gran's empty bed for the past few nights.

Which, I'm going to be absolutely honest with you, also didn't feel right. A bed without a warm human body isn't exactly the same thing. So back to Odelia and Chase we'd gone, and probably a good thing, too, for cats are natural predictors for life-threatening emergencies, so if something should happen in the middle of the night to warrant a run to the nearby hospital, we'd be the ones in the know and responsible for raising the alarm.

Now I know that having a baby isn't anywhere near the same thing as having your house catch fire or an earthquake ravaging your home, but it is still a major event.

"I can't sleep, Max," said Dooley, my best friend and compatriot.

"Me neither," I said, casting a baleful eye on the source of the trouble.

Odelia had taken to occasional groaning and moaning in the middle of the night, and getting up at all hours to go to the bathroom. Something to do with the pressure the baby was putting on her bladder. And each time Chase would wake up, cast a worried glance at his beloved, then reluctantly put his head down again and try to go back to sleep.

"Do you think this is going to be our life from now on?" asked Dooley. "Being kept awake all the time?"

"I doubt it," I said. "Once the baby is born things are bound to settle down again."

"I have heard that babies make a lot of noise, though," he said. "And that they don't care whether they do it in the middle of the night or the middle of the afternoon. They're very inconsiderate that way."

"I'm sure Odelia's baby won't be like that. He or she will

probably sleep all the time, just like we do, and won't be any trouble at all."

Dooley pondered these words, then decided to impart some more wisdom, as gleaned from one of the programs he likes to watch of an evening. "I've heard that babies can make the same noise as a jumbo jet. The racket is supposed to be deafening."

"Doubtful. No baby can make the sound of a jumbo jet. It's physically impossible."

"No, but it's true. They're so loud they have even invented special machines to muffle the sound. They're called baby monitors and people place them in the nursery and then make sure to close the door so the sound can't rupture their eardrums."

"You should really stop watching so much television, Dooley," I said. "It's starting to affect your common sense, if you ask me."

I'm usually not so hard on my friend, but lack of sleep has this effect on me: it makes me cranky.

And then when finally I had managed to doze off, Odelia's phone chimed and we all woke up with an annoyed groan.

"Who is it?" asked Chase sleepily as he rubbed his tired eyes.

"Dan," said Odelia, looking equally bleary-eyed. "Yes, Dan?" she spoke into the device. She listened for a few moments, then said, "All right, I'll be there," and hung up.

"What's wrong?" asked Chase.

"I don't know. Some emergency over at Fitchville."

"Fitchville? What's Fitchville?"

"It's what the locals have started calling the new compound Tab Fitch is building."

"The singer?"

"Yeah. He's been buying up houses and creating his own

private village. Safe to say his neighbors aren't too happy. There's been plenty of animosity about this building frenzy."

"So what happened? One of his neighbors took a potshot at him or something?"

"No idea. All Dan said was that something happened at Fitchville and to get out there as soon as possible."

"Want me to join you? In case things heat up?"

"No, I'll be fine," she said as she managed to get up with some effort. "Probably just some minor thing that Dan has decided to make a big deal of. You know what he's like."

"Here, I'll help you," said Chase as he rounded the bed and steadied her.

But she playfully slapped his hand away. "I'm perfectly capable of getting in and out of bed under my own steam, thank you very much."

"I know, but still..." He gave her a look of concern. "Maybe you should sit this one out?"

"I'm pregnant, not on the precipice of death, babe. I'll be fine."

Chase didn't look entirely convinced, but then Odelia does seem to overestimate her capacity to navigate everyday life movements ever since she's doubled in size. I know I wouldn't mind a helping paw when I had to carry that much excess weight around. But seeing she wasn't going to budge, he reluctantly backed off and went about his business.

We arrived downstairs, well ahead of our humans, and found Harriet and Brutus giggling on the couch for some unfathomable reason. They were staring at something on Harriet's tablet—and when I say Harriet's tablet I'm actually referring to the tablet Odelia has given to all of us, but since Harriet has been using it the most, its ownership seems to have quietly transferred to her.

"What are you guys looking at?" asked Dooley curiously.

"Only the most interesting thing ever invented," said Harriet.

"The wheel?" I asked. "The printing press? The light bulb?"

"Astrology," said Harriet. "Did you know that you can predict just about anything by simply looking at your horoscope once a day? For instance mine says that today I don't have to bother leaving the house since I'll only run into all kinds of trouble. Which means I won't leave the house, since these horoscopes never lie. What about you, Brutus?"

"Mine says that today is a fine day for some vigorous physical exercise. Have to keep that old ticker ticking over."

"You better go for a nice long walk then, sweetie pie. You don't want to ignore what the stars have in store for you."

"What about me?" asked Dooley eagerly. "What do the stars say about me?"

"Just that you should keep quiet," said Harriet, a touch harshly, I thought.

"Oh," said Dooley. "You mean..."

"Be quiet, Dooley, there's a good cat. Now Max, on the other hand," said Harriet, "has to watch out for strangers you meet on the street. Especially when they offer you candy."

"Don't take candy from a stranger, Max," said Brutus warningly.

"I don't eat candy," I said. "And as far as I remember no stranger has ever offered me any either. So your advice is pointless, Harriet. Where are you getting this from anyway?"

"Madame Burnett. It's a new site but it's getting rave reviews on Google."

"Well, then it hast to be good, doesn't it? Because Google never lies."

"Just you wait and see, Max," said Harriet. "Madame Burnett is never wrong."

"Yeah, yesterday she predicted I was going to see light at

the end of a long tunnel," said Brutus, "and when I got up to go to my litter box last night, I actually did see a light at the end of the corridor."

"That's the light Tex keeps burning so he doesn't tumble down the stairs when he gets up in the middle of the night," I said. "Though usually it's designed for kids, as anyone who's not Madame Burnett will tell you."

"Don't listen to him, tootsie roll," said Harriet. "Madame Burnett warns us about nasty skeptics, and clearly she was referring to Max."

Odelia was ready to head out, and now called for us to join her.

"Are you coming?" I asked.

"Haven't you heard a word I said?" said Harriet. "I can't leave the house today. Much too dangerous."

"And I need to get my morning exercise in," said Brutus.

"And I'm going to be quiet all day," Dooley murmured between closed lips.

And so shaking my head, I was off in Odelia's wake. Good thing I don't believe in all of that superstitious nonsense.

"Watch out for that candy, Max!" Harriet yelled after me. "Just say no!"

Chapter Two

I honestly didn't know what to expect. Mostly when we're called out to a place it's because some weird shenanigans have been going on, and more often than not dead bodies are involved. Today, though, no murders or other criminal activities had been reported. What had been reported was a cow that had accidentally stumbled into a pond. Though from the first report we got upon arrival, the 'accident' part was up for discussion.

"He did it on purpose!" the young man with the ginger

whiskers cried as he stood gesticulating in the direction of a nearby farm. "He pushed her in just as I was taking my morning swim!"

The young man reportedly was a famous pop singer, who had made a name for himself in recent years as an up-and-coming celebrity. Apart from his ginger hair, said ginger whiskers and a sizable pair of glasses he looked a little funny, though for the life of me I couldn't really put my finger on it. Not at first, at least. But then I got it: he was pretty short, but his legs were even shorter, which caused the disconcerting effect.

"So what are we looking at here?" asked Odelia. "A man pushed a cow into your swimming pool?"

"It's not a pool," said the young singer. "It's a duck pond, which I occasionally use to take a morning bath in. It's very invigorating for the body, and excellent for the skin."

We took a glance at the pond, which didn't look like any duck pond I'd ever seen. For one thing, it didn't contain a single duck. It also had a small dock and a diving board, and didn't have the kind of green scum that can usually be found floating on pond surfaces. This one had pristine water, colored an unnatural blue, and I could clearly smell the chlorine. It even had steps so you could get in and out of the 'pond' without any hassle.

The only thing, in fact, that made this pool different from your regular garden-variety backyard pool was the sizable cow standing in the middle of it, gazing at us with the kind of vaguely interested look that is typical for cows the world over. As if to say: honestly, I don't see what all the fuss is about, y'all.

"And look!" the irate little man continued, turning around, and we all looked where he was pointing. And now I saw it: his backside was liberally smeared with a sort of greenish-brownish substance. And as I took a sniff, immediately I knew what that substance was: cow dung. And as our eyes followed Mr. Fitch's, they landed on a nice round piece of similar dung on the edge of the pool, where presumably the cow had done its business preparatory to diving udder-first into the singer's pool.

Someone had clearly stepped into the cow dung, detracting somewhat from its perfect round shape and jellied consistency. Though what it lacked in substance had found a new destination on Tab Fitch's erstwhile clean trunks, which now stank to high heaven.

"I slipped," Tab explained when Odelia eyed him with marked curiosity.

"Better tell me the whole story from the beginning," she suggested.

Tab took a deep breath, and said, "First thing when I wake up, I always go in for half an hour of yoga. It's my way of starting the day. And then, to cool off, I jump into my pond."

"Only it's not really a pond, is it, Mr. Fitch? It looks more like a pool to me."

"Well, it's a pond," he insisted, "not a pool."

"Because you didn't get permission for a pool so you decided to push for a pond instead?" asked Odelia, who, like any reporter worth her salt, had done her research.

"Do we really have to go into all that again?" the singer lamented. "It's not important, is it? What's important is that I was floating in my pond when all of a sudden I heard a mooing sound, and when I opened my eyes, found myself looking at this huge... beast! It was standing next to the pond, staring at me intently, and then before I could stop it, it simply jumped into the pool and joined me! I mean, it almost jumped on top of me! If I hadn't swum out of the way it would have crushed me and I would have drowned!"

"Was there anyone else around when the cow jumped into the pool?" asked Odelia.

"No, there wasn't," the singer had to admit.

"So your assertion that the cow was pushed..."

"She was pushed—I have no idea how he did it, but there was definitely pushing involved. When have you ever heard of a cow spontaneously deciding to go for a swim?"

"Maybe she likes you? Felt an instant attraction and wanted to join you in the pool?"

He gave Odelia a dirty look. "It's not funny, Mrs. Kingsley. As far as I'm concerned this is attempted murder by cow, and I want you to know that I'm pressing charges."

"So what happened after you left the pool?"

"The pond!" he said, and made to stomp his foot on the grassy edge of the pond, before thinking better of it, since we were right next to the cow dung, and a stomp would have made quite a splash at this point. "Of course I scrambled to get out of the pond, only I hadn't seen the little 'present' the cow had left, so I stepped in it and slipped and fell."

Odelia laughed at this, then quickly covered it by coughing into her fist. "Are you going to press charges for attempted murder by cow dung?"

"Ha ha, very funny." The little man crossed his arms and scowled at the cow. "How am I going to get this animal out of my pond is what I'd like to know. Not to mention the damage its hoofs must have caused. Probably trampled so hard in her panic at being shoved in that she kicked a hole in the floor, causing the water to start draining away."

"Chlorinated water and farmland don't go together well, sir," said Odelia. "You might be looking at some environmental charges yourself if word gets out about your... pond."

Now he turned his scowl on her. "I should have known that you'd simply come out here to mock me and to gloat at my misfortune." He wagged a reproachful finger in her direction. "Well, let me tell you one thing, missy. I'm the sole source of a lot of business coming this way, and a lot of new jobs. So you can laugh all you want, but the council loves me, and when I tell them what happened here today, Plontek won't know what hit him!"

And with these words, and a final withering glance at the cow, he stalked off, scratching his backside as he did, before remembering it was covered in muck.

"Where's that little fella going, then?" asked the cow now.

"Home, I guess," I said. "To freshen up."

"Pity. I was starting to like him. Funny little guy."

"What's your name, by the way?" I asked. "For the article," I clarified. "Important to get these details right and avoid rectifications and letters to the editor later on."

"Bella," said the cow. "Not very original, I know, but then Dunton isn't one for originality."

"That would be Dunton Plontek, your owner?" I asked.

"That's right. He's the one who told me to take a plunge this morning."

"And nudged you?"

"Oh, sure. Do you really think I'd jump into this here pool because I wanted to? I hate getting wet, cat, as I'm sure you of all creatures will understand."

"Oh, yes," I said, as I studied the water with a marked shiver.

"It's supposed to be invigorating," said Dooley. "Though I prefer to stay dry myself."

"So how did he get you to dive into this here pool?" I asked.

"He threw in my feed," said Bella. "All wet and chewy it was, too. Not very nice of him."

"He threw in your feed?" I asked, marveling at the ingenuity of this Mr. Plontek.

"Absolutely. Lay a trail all the way from the stable to here, and then once I was out here he took aim and threw in the rest. He also gave me a prod in the rear, which caused me to have that little accident that you see there. The little fella that was floating in the pool probably didn't notice, but then he wouldn't have, since Dunton made sure he couldn't be seen, lying flat on his belly as he did." She glanced idly in the direction of the farm, whose roof could be seen rising up behind some trees beyond. "He probably skedaddled it back the moment I landed in the pool with a big splash." She shook her head. "Nasty rotten trick he pulled on me. I hate it when my food gets all soggy. I like it fresh and crispy."

And as I related all this to Odelia, she smiled widely throughout the whole sordid tale.

"So now the big question is," said Bella, eyeing me sadly, "how am I going to get out of this mess?"

Chapter Three

Tab's wife Madison knew better than to laugh when she saw her husband storm into the house and up the stairs. He'd been locked into a fight with the neighbors for the past year, and while he'd managed to square almost all of them, Dunton Plontek proved the one most difficult to conciliate.

The Plonteks had owned the farm next door for generations, and weren't as easily encouraged by the promise of a big monetary reward as the other neighbors, who had at some point all accepted Tab's offer and sold their properties and moved away. And in so doing had made Tab's dream come true: to create his own small domain in the countryside, right on the outskirts of Hampton Cove, the town he'd grown up in and so had she, and live peacefully without being bothered by what the neighbors thought.

Now Tab could play his music as loud as he wanted, or throw parties all night long, or splash around in his pool without being seen or heard by anyone.

Except Dunton, who refused to sell, and had, by the looks

of things, managed to play a practical joke on her husband that morning, by infesting his pool with a bovine intruder.

"I'm going to take a shower," Tab muttered darkly before taking the stairs two at a time. She decided to follow him up, since she had some unfinished business to take care of. Some very important unfinished business, which she hoped to settle today.

And so it was with a spring in her step that she followed her husband into the bathroom. A spring, but also the fear that her hopes would be thwarted once again.

So she took out the device, assumed the position and hoped for the best.

Tab, meanwhile, was already in the walk-in shower, having divested himself of his soiled trunks, and deftly scrubbing away the last remnants of his cow encounter.

As she waited for the result to finally show, she had to still her beating heart, and a sudden sense of panic rushed through her, almost making her feel nauseous.

It had to work—it just had to. But when she finally screwed up the courage to look, she saw that once again… it hadn't.

She released a whimper of disappointment.

Tab, stepping out of the shower, caught sight of the pregnancy test. And when he saw the look on her face, immediately enveloped her into his arms. "Next time, babe," he said quietly, gently caressing her back. "We'll just keep on trying, won't we?"

She nodded wordlessly, not even bothered by the fact that he'd made her front all wet. And when he finally let go, she sank down on the toilet seat and studied the test for a few more minutes, as if by looking the result would change, then threw it in the trash can under the sink.

A knock at the door took her out of her reverie, and she was glad for it. She had a tendency to allow dark thoughts to envelop her and drag her down, and this week of all weeks she couldn't afford that kind of behavior.

They had guests, after all, and plenty of them.

Tab had just started recording his new album in his private recording studio, and so his producer was staying at the compound, and so were Tab's cousin, who was shooting a movie about the making of the record, and of course Tab's best friend since kindergarten, Saul Goff. With so many people and the responsibility of the new album, the atmosphere had been electric for days, even without cow-related incidents thrown into the mix.

"Have you had breakfast yet?" asked Tab as he towel-dried his hair.

She shook her head. "Just some fruit and yogurt."

"Have the others eaten?"

"Waiting for you, I think."

"Well, let's not keep them waiting. I want to get started as soon as possible." He glanced at her through the mirror. "Sunroom, you think? Or outside on the deck?"

"Outside is fine. It's a nice day for it."

The trouble with having multiple houses and locations is how to choose where to sit down for meals. It was a luxury, of course, but it still took some organizing. The bigger their property grew, the more maintenance, which is why they urgently needed to hire a manager to handle that part, and also a crew of people to keep things running smoothly.

She now became aware of how wet her shirt actually was, and walked out and into the bedroom to put on a dry one. She'd planned to head into town that morning, and leave Tab and the others to go about their business of laying down some new music tracks.

And she'd just changed into a fresh shirt when she overheard some harsh words being exchanged. The voices were drifting in from a nearby room. And as she listened, she recognized Saul's voice and Tab's, as they seemed to be in the throes of an argument.

It was rare for the two old friends to fight, but not surprising, considering the pressure Tab was under. The record company was expecting an album that would sell at least as well or preferably even better than the last one, which had been a number-one hit all around the world, spawning several big hits and turning Tab Fitch into a global star.

Numerous rewards, a sold-out tour, and all the craziness and attention that went with it had heaped on the pressure to prove he wasn't a one-hit wonder but an artist who was here to stay.

It had caused Tab a lot of sleepless nights over the past couple of months. Which is why Madison hadn't wanted to trouble him with her own problems. Even though he wanted to start a family as much as she did, he had other stuff on his mind right now.

She decided to slip out unseen, not wanting her husband or his best friend to know they'd been overheard, and soon was on her way into town.

And she'd already traveled a mile before she remembered she'd promised Tab they'd breakfast together—them and the rest of the crew.

Oh, well. She was sure they could manage without her.

ABOUT NIC

Nic has a background in political science and before being struck by the writing bug worked odd jobs around the world (including but not limited to massage therapist in Mexico, gardener in Italy, restaurant manager in India, and Berlitz teacher in Belgium).

When he's not writing he enjoys curling up with a good (comic) book, watching British crime dramas, French comedies or Nancy Meyers movies, sampling pastry (apple cake!), pasta and chocolate (preferably the dark variety), twisting himself into a pretzel doing morning yoga, going for a run, and spoiling his big red tomcat Tommy.

He lives with his wife (and aforementioned cat) in a small village smack dab in the middle of absolutely nowhere and is probably writing his next 'Mysteries of Max' book right now.

www.nicsaint.com

ALSO BY NIC SAINT

The Mysteries of Max

Purrfect Murder

Purrfectly Deadly

Purrfect Revenge

Purrfect Heat

Purrfect Crime

Purrfect Rivalry

Purrfect Peril

Purrfect Secret

Purrfect Alibi

Purrfect Obsession

Purrfect Betrayal

Purrfectly Clueless

Purrfectly Royal

Purrfect Cut

Purrfect Trap

Purrfectly Hidden

Purrfect Kill

Purrfect Boy Toy

Purrfectly Dogged

Purrfectly Dead

Purrfect Saint

Purrfect Advice

Purrfect Passion

A Purrfect Gnomeful

Purrfect Cover

Purrfect Patsy

Purrfect Son

Purrfect Fool

Purrfect Fitness

Purrfect Setup

Purrfect Sidekick

Purrfect Deceit

Purrfect Ruse

Purrfect Swing

Purrfect Cruise

Purrfect Harmony

Purrfect Sparkle

Purrfect Cure

Purrfect Cheat

Purrfect Catch

Purrfect Design

Purrfect Life

Purrfect Thief

Purrfect Crust

Purrfect Bachelor

Purrfect Double

Purrfect Date

Purrfect Hit

The Mysteries of Max Box Sets

Box Set 1 (Books 1-3)

Box Set 2 (Books 4-6)

Box Set 3 (Books 7-9)

Box Set 4 (Books 10-12)

Box Set 5 (Books 13-15)

Box Set 6 (Books 16-18)

Box Set 7 (Books 19-21)

Box Set 8 (Books 22-24)

Box Set 9 (Books 25-27)

Box Set 10 (Books 28-30)

Box Set 11 (Books 31-33)

Box Set 12 (Books 34-36)

Box Set 13 (Books 37-39)

Box Set 14 (Books 40-42)

Box Set 15 (Books 43-45)

The Mysteries of Max Big Box Sets

Big Box Set 1 (Books 1-10)

Big Box Set 2 (Books 11-20)

The Mysteries of Max Shorts

Purrfect Santa (3 shorts in one)

Purrfectly Flealess

Purrfect Wedding

Nora Steel

Murder Retreat

The Kellys

Murder Motel

Death in Suburbia

Emily Stone

Murder at the Art Class

Washington & Jefferson

First Shot

Alice Whitehouse

Spooky Times

Spooky Trills

Spooky End

Spooky Spells

Ghosts of London

Between a Ghost and a Spooky Place

Public Ghost Number One

Ghost Save the Queen

Box Set 1 (Books 1-3)

A Tale of Two Harrys

Ghost of Girlband Past

Ghostlier Things

Charleneland

Deadly Ride

Final Ride

Neighborhood Witch Committee

Witchy Start

Witchy Worries

Witchy Wishes

Saffron Diffley

Crime and Retribution

Vice and Verdict

Felonies and Penalties (Saffron Diffley Short 1)

The B-Team

Once Upon a Spy

Tate-à-Tate

Enemy of the Tates

Ghosts vs. Spies

The Ghost Who Came in from the Cold

Witchy Fingers

Witchy Trouble

Witchy Hexations

Witchy Possessions

Witchy Riches

Box Set 1 (Books 1-4)

The Mysteries of Bell & Whitehouse

One Spoonful of Trouble

Two Scoops of Murder

Three Shots of Disaster

Box Set 1 (Books 1-3)

A Twist of Wraith

A Touch of Ghost

A Clash of Spooks

Box Set 2 (Books 4-6)

The Stuffing of Nightmares

A Breath of Dead Air

An Act of Hodd

Box Set 3 (Books 7-9)

A Game of Dons

Standalone Novels

When in Bruges

The Whiskered Spy

ThrillFix

Homejacking

The Eighth Billionaire

The Wrong Woman

Made in the USA
Las Vegas, NV
29 August 2023

76819582R00121